"I have a right to know," she said.

"Are you sure about that?"

"I said it, didn't I?" Rae uttered the words like a challenge and tossed her head, sending her hair flying over her shoulder.

Sully inclined his head, a hint of a smile slowly making its way across his lips.

"That you did," he agreed.

It felt as if time had suddenly stopped, the moment freezing around the only two people who were in the room. For now, the only two people in the world. Then, when time finally began to thaw out, everything that happened from then on did so in crystal clear slow motion.

Even her heart had stopped. And then, when it began to beat again, it wasn't hammering wildly; it beat to some lyrical rhythm that she wasn't aware of ever having heard before. She was aware of it now. Very aware of it. Very aware of him.

And very aware of his lips when they finally came down on hers.

* * *

Be sure to check out the next books in this excit miniseries:

Cavanaugh Justi al

If you're or
think of Harlequin
#harlequinromsuspense

D0818477

Dear Reader,

My beloved editor and I decided to try something new this time around (actually, it was her idea and I said, "Sure"). What you have before you is a melding of the Cavanaugh Justice series and the Forever, Texas series. You get a taste of both series and hopefully that will pique your interest about the people of Forever.

Sully Cavanaugh has just finally closed a serial killer case after spending more than eighteen months tracking the killer down. The case costs him, putting his faith in humanity seriously to the test. And he needs a change of scenery and a change in his way of life. His great-uncle Seamus makes arrangements for Sully to stay—and work—at the small horse ranch in Forever, Texas.

It's just the change Sully is looking for, especially when the ranch foreman turns out to be Rae Mulcahy, an all-around wrangler who is very easy on the eyes. But trouble seems to follow Sully wherever he goes and it isn't too long before another ranch hand goes missing. It's up to Sully to find out what happened. Things get complicated when Rae insists on taking part in the investigation—and they discover that the ranch hand wasn't who he said he was.

As ever, I thank you for taking the time to pick up one of my stories, and from the bottom of my heart, I wish you someone to love who loves you back.

All the best,

Marie Ferrarella

CAVANAUGH COWBOY

Marie Ferrarella

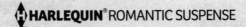

HARLEQUIN® ROMANTIC SUSPENSE

Recycling programs
for this product may
not exist in your area.

ISBN-13: 978-1-335-66198-2

Cavanaugh Cowboy

Copyright © 2019 by Marie Rydzynski-Ferrarella

This edition published by arrangement with Harlequin Books S.A.

For questions and comments about the quality of this book, please contact us at CustomerService@Harlequin.com.

® and TM are trademarks of Harlequin Enterprises Limited or its corporate affiliates. Trademarks indicated with ® are registered in the United States Patent and Trademark Office, the Canadian Intellectual Property Office and in other countries.

Printed in U.S.A.

USA TODAY bestselling and RITA® Award–winning author **Marie Ferrarella** has written more than two hundred and fifty books for Harlequin, some under the name Marie Nicole. Her romances are beloved by fans worldwide. Visit her website, marieferrarella.com.

Books by Marie Ferrarella

Harlequin Romantic Suspense

Cavanaugh Justice

Mission: Cavanaugh Baby
Cavanaugh on Duty
A Widow's Guilty Secret
Cavanaugh's Surrender
Cavanaugh Rules
Cavanaugh's Bodyguard
Cavanaugh Fortune
How to Seduce a Cavanaugh
Cavanaugh or Death
Cavanaugh Cold Case
Cavanaugh in the Rough
Cavanaugh on Call
Cavanaugh Encounter
Cavanaugh Vanguard
Cavanaugh Cowboy

Visit the Author Profile page at
Harlequin.com for more titles.

To
Jessica,
Who Still Hasn't Read
A Single One Of These.
All My Love,
Mom

Prologue

"Something wrong, boy?" Seamus Cavanaugh asked. He was the long-retired police chief and currently the head of a small but thriving security firm, as well as the official patriarch of an extremely large clan that was firmly entrenched in the law enforcement community. He lowered himself into a love seat beside Sullivan Cavanaugh, one of his nephew Angus's sons.

Angus was one of his late younger brother Murdoch's sons. Despite the fact that there were enough Cavanaughs within Aurora, California, to populate their own small town, and Seamus was far from spending his days sipping a scotch and watching shadows elongate themselves across his front porch, he felt it his duty to watch over each and every one of them. From the oldest—his son Andrew, a retired police chief like himself—to the youngest, Dugan and Toni's daughter, who was about to reach her first birthday, Seamus took an interest in all of them.

At first, Sullivan Cavanaugh didn't realize that his great-uncle was speaking to him. There were a lot of people at this gathering and consequently a lot of noise. It was another one of his uncle Andrew's typical impromptu gatherings—nobody cooked like Uncle Andrew—and every inch of the house and grounds was stuffed with members of the Cavanaugh family as well as other friends, all of whom, in one way or another, dedicated their lives to keeping the good citizens of Aurora safe.

Sully had hoped that coming here would be enough to erase this burned-out feeling he'd been carrying around, a feeling that had unexpectedly descended over him even as he had wound up almost eighteen months' worth of following cold leads and circular trails before finally finding the murderer he'd been so relentlessly pursuing.

Usually, once a case was put to bed, he would feel buoyed up, invigorated and ready to start again on a new case.

But not this time.

This time, the burned-out feeling remained, growing only more oppressive, preventing him from going on.

Still, he hadn't thought it was that obvious.

Sully blinked, shifting his body toward his great-uncle.

"Nothing's wrong, sir," he answered, doing his best not to sound the way he felt.

Steel-gray eyebrows drew together over exceedingly penetrating dark eyes.

"Don't give me that, boy. I've seen that look before. You just solved the Gilmore case, didn't you?" It was a rhetorical question.

"My team and I did, yes," Sully replied.

Everyone in the room was aware of that, he thought. Aware, too, that it had been a team effort even though for some reason, Sully felt unaccountably alone at this point. He wasn't accustomed to feeling this way.

"That was rather an important case," Seamus commented. "Even the mayor took an interest in it. And yet here you are, looking like your favorite dog just died."

Sully shrugged. "I guess it's all those long hours finally catching up to me. Maybe I just need to go home and get some rest."

But Seamus didn't appear convinced.

"It's more than that," the onetime police chief said. Seamus scrutinized the man seated beside him in silence for a moment before asking, "Burnout?"

There was no sense in lying, Sully thought. Even though he was in his early seventies, the old man was too sharp to try to fool.

"I guess maybe," Sully acknowledged with a careless shrug. "But I'll get over it." He said it more to convince his great-uncle than himself.

"I'm sure you will," Seamus told him with the

confidence of a man who had seen and lived through a great deal in his lifetime. "But in the meantime, maybe you need a little extra help."

"Extra help?" Sully repeated, not sure what his great-uncle was telling him.

His guess was that the man was going to suggest possibly a temporary closer acquaintance with Johnnie Walker.

But he didn't.

Instead, Seamus nodded and said, "A change of scenery."

Sully didn't see how that could help and dismissed the suggestion. "I'm not sure if a vacation—"

Seamus continued as if Sully hadn't said anything. "What do you think about Texas?"

"Texas?" Sully echoed. He'd never been to that state, nor did he have any desire to change that. "I don't really think anything about Texas," he began but just like before, he got no further.

"I have this old friend who runs a diner in Forever, Texas. She's also got this small horse ranch," Seamus told him. "I'm sure if I contact her, Miss Joan'll let you stay there."

Sully looked at his great-uncle, bemused. Everyone knew that the man could be a bit eccentric.

"You call your old friend Miss Joan?" Sully questioned.

Seamus saw nothing unusual about that. "Everyone does," he said. "All I have to do is pick up a phone and call her—"

"That's okay, really," Sully replied, cutting his

great-uncle off. He began to rise. "I don't need a change of scenery."

Seamus caught his wrist. For a man in his seventies, he had an exceptionally strong grip. Sully sank back down.

"Yes," Seamus insisted with emphasis, "you do. And as I seem to recall, wide-open spaces don't intimidate you. You ride, don't you?"

The old man's memory was as sharp as Uncle Andrew's. And, like all his uncles, he also had all the answers before he asked the questions, so there was no point in pretending that he didn't know his way around a horse, Sully thought. He did. Riding tended to relax him. That went all the way back to his childhood and summers spent with his father, enjoying wide-open spaces.

"Yes, sir, I do."

"Good," Seamus pronounced. "Nothing left to do but pack your bag."

Sully eyed the older man uncertainly. Seamus was assuming a lot here.

"But you haven't even called your friend yet," he pointed out.

Seamus leaned in closer to him.

"The good thing about old friends, Sully," Seamus said in a low, confidential voice, "is that you know their answer even before you ask the question. Another good thing is that you can always count on them for a favor." As he sat back, the older man's smile widened. "Now, stop arguing with me, boy, and pack your bag."

Chapter 1

Miss Joan knew the minute that Sully Cavanaugh walked into her establishment.

She wasn't looking toward the diner's entrance at the time, but she saw the suddenly dazed expressions of utter admiration on her waitresses' faces. The two young women, Mandy and Beth, appeared to have been suddenly struck speechless.

Mandy recovered first. Sighing deeply, the dark-haired young woman murmured, "That is one tall, cool drink of water." Sheer appreciation rang in her voice.

"There'll be no sipping from that glass," Miss Joan informed both the young women sternly. "He's the great-nephew of a friend of mine."

"I'll say he's great," Beth pronounced with enthusiasm.

Miss Joan frowned and waved the two young women toward their work areas. "You two have tables to bus," Miss Joan reminded the mesmerized duo. "I suggest that you get to them before the piles get too large."

As a police detective, Sully was used to walking into unfamiliar places, his every footstep carefully observed, with only seconds for him to assess whether or not his life was in jeopardy. This situation wasn't that serious, but he was still aware of the fact that he was being closely scrutinized.

Probably because he was a stranger, Sully guessed. From what he'd gathered from his great-uncle, Forever was, for the most part, a small, tightly knit community.

The thin older woman at the counter made him think of an eagle, dissecting his every step as he drew closer to her. She was trim, narrow shouldered and a redhead, most likely a natural one once, but given her age, he guessed that she sought out a little artificial help to maintain the deep red color.

She'd been beautiful once, he thought. And he could see that back in the day, she had definitely been the type who had caught his great-uncle's eye.

"Excuse me," Sully said, clearing his throat.

The redheaded woman looked at him, and then at his hat.

Belatedly, he remembered to take off the black Stetson that his great-uncle had gifted him with when he'd left Aurora, bound for Forever. He wasn't accustomed to wearing a hat, but the sun outside made it almost a necessity.

Running the brim along his fingers, he said, "I'm looking for Miss Joan."

Miss Joan stopped wiping down the small counter space directly in front of her. Leaning slightly forward on the hand that was against the counter, she informed him, "You found her."

Sully put out his hand. "I'm Sully Cavanaugh. I think that my great-uncle called you to say that I was coming out."

Miss Joan glanced down at the offered hand but waited a beat before finally shaking it.

"No, he said he was *sending* you out for your own good," she corrected. "He said something about you needing a place to regroup."

Sully was accustomed to being a private person and waiting before offering any information beyond the bare minimum. This woman already seemed to know more about him than he was happy about.

"I don't know about that—"

"He did," Miss Joan continued, cutting him off. Hazel-green eyes slowly slid over the length of his torso, making no secret of the fact that she was assessing what she saw. "You look a lot like Seamus," she told him. "Back when he was young and good-looking," she added. "I imagine he's rather old, craggy and fat by now." Her voice rose slightly at the end of her statement, a silent invitation to be contradicted.

"He's still pretty trim," Sully told her. "And I think he sees himself as wise, not craggy."

"But he is old," Miss Joan said, noticing that the young man before her hadn't said anything to contradict that.

"Old?" Sully corrected that impression now. "Not so you'd notice."

Miss Joan waved a hand at his words. "You're his family. You have to say that."

Rather than protest, Sully took out his cell phone. He pressed the app where he kept family photographs and found the one he'd taken of his great-uncle earlier in the year.

He held it up for her to view. "Judge for yourself, Miss Joan."

Rather than taking the phone from him, she took hold of Sully's hand to steady it. Miss Joan peered intently at the photograph he had pulled up.

She pursed her lips and asked suspiciously, "When was this taken?"

Sully thought for a moment. "Around the first of the year."

Her eyes narrowed, looking at him like a seasoned interrogator. "*This* year?"

"Yes, ma'am."

"My, my," she murmured under her breath, releasing his hand. "If I wasn't already spoken for, I might think about looking Seamus up again, see if some of that old magic was still there."

Sully slipped the phone back into his pocket. "Old magic?" he echoed.

Although Sully had always considered himself to be pretty open-minded, it was hard picturing someone his great-uncle's age having anything that even remotely resembled a love life.

Miss Joan gave him a somewhat impatient look. "Use your imagination, boy. I'm not going to spell it out for you," she informed him. "I'm a lady."

Sully chose to avoid the subject altogether by changing it. "You and Uncle Seamus have the same way of addressing me."

Miss Joan raised her eyes to the handsome, rugged young stranger's face.

"I'll let you in on a secret. Saying 'boy' is a lot easier than remembering everyone's names. Although I do," the woman added authoritatively as a coda, just in case he thought she didn't.

Sully smiled at this woman who apparently had once known his great-uncle extremely well. "I never doubted it, ma'am."

Miss Joan surprised him by frowning. "Don't keep calling me ma'am," she chided. "Makes me feel like I'm a thousand years old."

"No way, ma'—Miss Joan." Denying her assumption, Sully quickly corrected himself before he wound up slipping again.

She nodded. "Keep practicing, boy. Meanwhile, sit down and take a load off," she instructed, nodding at the stool that was directly to his right. When he did as he was told, she pulled out a menu from beneath the counter and slid it directly in front of him. "What'll you have? We're serving lunch, but I can have Angel whip up breakfast for you if you'd rather have that."

Sully didn't bother looking at the menu. He left it right where it was. "No need to go to any trouble," he told Miss Joan. "I just wanted to stop by to say thank you and to pay my respects—"

"If you want to pay your respects," Miss Joan informed him, cutting Sully off, "you'll eat something like I said. Can't have you wandering off with an empty belly." She stopped and peered at him. "What are you grinning about?"

Sully did a little self-editing before answering the woman. "Uncle Seamus said you had a way about you."

Miss Joan laughed and took a guess at the exchange between Seamus and his great-nephew.

"Probably said I was like a stubborn mule," she corrected. Seeing that Sully was about to deny her assumption, she said, "And he's right. I am. So stop sitting there, giving me lip, and order something. The sooner you eat, the sooner we can get you out to the ranch."

"Then I *can* stay there?" Sully asked.

He knew that his great-uncle had said that the woman had extended the invitation, but Sully still had his doubts that the invitation had actually been tendered. He really didn't want to impose if she didn't want him staying at the ranch. After all, from start to finish, this had all been Seamus's idea, not his.

"That's what Seamus and I agreed on," Miss Joan replied with an air of finality. And then her eyes bored into the young man before her. "Why, you change your mind about staying?"

"No, ma'—Miss Joan." Sully caught himself at the last moment again. "It's just that I am surprised," he admitted.

"How so?" Miss Joan asked.

She was aware that not just her two waitresses, but almost everyone within the diner at this point was paying attention to this handsome, dark-haired young man with the liquid green eyes. That he was oblivious to the attention he was garnering spoke well of him.

"You don't know me from Adam," Sully replied. He was used to friendly people, but they all knew him. This situation was different.

"Maybe I don't," Miss Joan admitted. "But I know Seamus, and he wouldn't send me someone who wasn't trustworthy, even if that someone turned out to be a relative of his." And that was that in her book. "You got any other doubts that you're wrestling with that I can put to rest?"

A small hint of a smile curved the corners of Sully's mouth. He shook his head. "None."

"Okay, then," Miss Joan declared. "Let's get your order out of the way and then, while Angel makes it for you, you can tell me all about what that sly devil of a man is up to these days."

Sully had a feeling that once he got back to Aurora, Seamus would ask him the same questions about Miss Joan. "Well, Uncle Seamus said to be sure to thank you for putting me up."

Miss Joan waved a thin, slightly blue-veined hand dismissively.

"He already said that on the phone when he called. I'm interested in what he'd been doing for the last forty years before that phone call." Then, because he didn't begin to immediately answer, Miss Joan switched subjects like a rerouted runaway train and nodded at the menu she had placed in front of him. "Made up your mind yet?"

The woman jumped around from topic to topic like a frog landing on hot lily pads, Sully thought. But even though he'd been in her company for less than ten minutes, he knew better than to make that observation to her. So instead, he made his selection.

"I'll have today's special," he told Miss Joan, pushing the menu to the side.

Miss Joan didn't bother turning the menu around. Though it changed every day, she knew the selections by heart.

"Mandy," she called over her shoulder, "tell Angel we need her special." She fixed Sully with a look. "Rare, medium or well-done?"

He preferred rare, but he knew that to some cooks, that meant almost raw, so he went the safe route. "Medium."

Miss Joan nodded, obviously approving his selection. "Good choice," she pronounced. Glancing at the waitress she'd summoned, she saw that the young woman seemed rooted to the floor. Mandy was staring at Sully as if he was the most tempting ice cream sundae she had ever encountered. "Well, you heard the man, Mandy. Get a move on."

Coming to, Mandy mumbled, "Yes, Miss Joan." The brunette spun on her heel and made her way through the kitchen's double doors.

Miss Joan didn't bother suppressing the sigh that escaped her lips. There were times when the young women she took under her wing and into her employ could be a trial.

Turning back to Sully, she said, "All right, that gives us a little time to kill. Tell me what that old man's been up to."

The diner had slowly been filling up since he'd first walked in. Sully was aware of the way each and every one of the patrons who came in stared at him before they went to either a booth or one of the stools at the counter. But more than that, he was aware of their growing number.

"Don't you have to see to your patrons?" he asked Miss Joan, hoping to redirect her attention toward something else.

The expression on Miss Joan's face told him she knew exactly what he was up to. And she had an answer for that.

"I own this place, Sully. That means that I get to do what I want whenever I want—within reason. Since I've got two girls taking orders and bringing them back, plus a third girl coming in about fifteen minutes from now, that means that right now, I get to ask questions and find out what that old Romeo is doing these days."

"Romeo?" Sully repeated incredulously.

He had been just about to take a sip of the coffee Miss Joan had poured for him, and now he was glad that he hadn't. Otherwise he was certain that he would have wound up choking on it. Or, at the very least, spitting that coffee out in a spray and making unplanned, unwanted contact with the man he'd just glanced at sitting on his left.

"Your great-uncle," Miss Joan clarified. "He might look like a harmless old man to you, but unless I miss my guess, there's nothing harmless about him." She fixed Sully with a deep, probing look. "Am I right?"

She had that right, Sully thought, recalling Seamus's recent history. His great-uncle was more active than men half his age.

"Well, he gave retirement a try," he told Miss Joan. "But then a few years back he showed up on Uncle Andrew's doorstep one evening, saying that he just really wasn't the retiring type and what he really wanted was to get back in the game."

Miss Joan didn't seem surprised by the revelation. Despite her earlier question, she had never envisioned Seamus Cavanaugh quietly sitting in a rocking chair, watching life passing him by.

"And did he?" she asked.

"Well, since he couldn't get back into the police department because of his age, he decided to start up his own firm," Sully told the older woman. "At first, it was going to be a detective agency, but he realized that that might require a lot of stealth, undercover work and although he really hated to admit it, he wasn't as quick or as spry on his feet as he once was. Running a security firm suited his needs far better."

Miss Joan's deep, rich laugh echoed through the diner. "That sounds just like Seamus," she said with something that sounded like affection. And then her tone shifted just a little as she asked Sully, "So what does his wife have to say about this newest undertaking of his?"

"Nothing," Sully answered. He saw Miss Joan's expertly drawn-in eyebrows rise in a silent query, so he answered her question before she asked it. "His wife died more than ten years ago. That's what prompted him to pack up and go live in a retirement community to start with. But a few years into that, Uncle Seamus decided that kind of life was just too stagnant for him."

"Humph," Miss Joan reflected. "A retirement community would be too inert and soul killing for a man like Seamus," she declared. She leaned in a little closer again. "So, how's his firm doing? Really."

His great-uncle had just taken on another operative and he was still turning away business. Sully had to admit that the man was happier than he'd seen him in a long while. But that was something for Seamus to share with Miss Joan on his own.

So Sully just replied, "Keeps him busy."

Miss Joan nodded, thinking. "Maybe once you've sorted out whatever it is that brought you down here, Harry and I will invite Seamus to come on out for a visit."

"Harry?" For a moment, Sully drew a blank. Was this someone in Forever, or from Seamus's past?

"My husband," Miss Joan clarified, adding, "the man who finally wore me down and pushed a ring on my finger. Technically, the ranch you'll be staying on is Harry's. But the man's got no more use for it than I do. So now we've got a foreman running things, and every once in a while," she added like a recently remembered footnote, "we sell one of the horses bred there."

Mandy appeared at her elbow with a tray. "Angel sent out the lunch you asked for."

"I didn't ask for it. He did," Miss Joan corrected. Taking the tray from the waitress, the diner owner quickly distributed what was on there and placed it in front of Sully. "Here's your lunch, boy. Hope it meets with your expectations."

The statement was politely worded, but there was no mistaking the confidence that was behind it. Miss Joan was expecting nothing short of a euphoric response from the first forkful to the last.

Well, Sully thought, half amused, half bemused, he could always fake it if need be.

He cut into the steak and eased the first piece into his mouth while Miss Joan watched him, waiting for his response.

When flavor exploded in his mouth, he was slightly surprised and deeply relieved.

"It's good," he told his great-uncle's friend.

"Of course it's good," Miss Joan answered. "I

told you it would be. Were you expecting that it wouldn't be?"

"No, Miss Joan," Sully answered politely, "I wasn't expecting anything else except what you said."

Miss Joan merely smiled, knowing that he was humoring her. But given who he was and who his great-uncle was, she didn't mind. She nodded her head. "You'll do, boy. You'll do."

Chapter 2

Miss Joan smiled and nodded with approval as she cleared away the empty plates.

"Well, for a man who didn't want to eat anything, you certainly did justice to that steak and apple pie," she commented, then swiped a cloth along the counter, getting rid of any lingering crumbs. Finished, she asked, "Can I get you anything else?"

"Only if you want to watch me explode," Sully answered.

He placed his hand against his stomach as if he was trying to keep the contents inside from suddenly emerging.

"Wouldn't want to see that," Miss Joan told him with a puckered expression. "All right then, if you can wait here for a while—no more than an hour—

Harry said he can come by and bring you up to the J-H Ranch."

Sully saw no reason why he needed to be taken by the hand and escorted. "I don't want to put you out any further," he told Miss Joan. "I'm sure I can find the ranch on my own. Just point me in the right direction and tell me approximately how many miles the ranch is from here."

The lines along Miss Joan's forehead furrowed, forming a skeptical pucker.

"Are you sure?" she asked. She was used to townspeople finding their way around, but this was a tenderfoot, and she had no knowledge about his innate skills. "Because Harry won't mind. The man loves company and he loves to talk. Says he doesn't get much practice with me around. Something about sucking up all the oxygen in the room," she added, shaking her head and dismissing her husband's words.

"Yes, I'm sure," Sully told her. He noticed that Mandy reached under the counter to take the dishes that Miss Joan had cleared away. The waitress lingered just long enough to look at him longingly. "Once I get settled in, I would love to meet with your husband, Miss Joan, but right now, I'm anxious to see where I'll be hanging my hat for the next few weeks."

"You're not just going to be hanging your hat," Miss Joan informed him. She eyed Sully, trying to decide if he was just talking or if he was serious. If it was the latter, he needed to be set straight. "You understand that you're going to be working for your keep once you're at the ranch. My foreman doesn't have much patience with people who don't pull their own weight or are waiting to be served," she told Sully.

"Oh, I understand," he answered, not wanting there to be any misunderstandings. "Uncle Seamus made the terms of this arrangement very clear, and to be honest, I'm really looking forward to working with my hands."

Miss Joan studied him for a moment, decided he was being honest and then nodded. "All right then, about those directions you wanted."

Flipping over the menu she had just used earlier, Miss Joan took out the pencil she had in her apron pocket. Using a minimum of strokes, she drew a very basic map for Sully that took him from the center of the town to edge of the ranch that she and Harry owned.

Finished, she put the pencil back into her pocket with a flourish and let him have the map.

"You sure you don't want to wait for Harry?" she asked, looking at him somewhat dubiously.

"No, this'll do fine," Sully assured her, tapping the map she had drawn for him.

Miss Joan had never accepted anything at face value. This was no exception. "How often do you get lost?"

"I don't," he said simply. "I just keep on going until I get there."

Her expression was only partially skeptical at this point.

"All the same, I wouldn't want to be the one responsible for losing one of Seamus's great-grand-kids, even if he does have a bunch of them to spare," Miss Joan said.

"You won't be." His tone was final, indicating that the discussion was at an end. Sully reached into his pocket again, this time to take out his wallet. He was about to flip the folded leather open. "How much do I owe you for lunch?"

Miss Joan's face darkened, like clouds gathering in the sky just before a storm. "You take your hand out of your pocket, boy, or your journey's going to be over before it ever gets started," she warned him. Under her watchful eye, Sully did as he was told—for now. "Nothing was said about there being a charge for lunch."

Still, Sully's hand lingered by his pocket. "I'd feel better paying my own way."

"And I'd feel better if I were twenty years younger, but we can't all get what we wish for," Miss Joan snapped. "Now get going. And be sure to tell Rae I sent you."

"Ray?" Sully asked.

Miss Joan nodded. "That's the foreman. Rae Mulcahy. Otherwise you might find yourself being shot for trespassing."

He should have known, Sully thought. People out here stripped things down to the basics.

"Right. I'll introduce myself first thing," he promised the woman. "Thank you for lunch, Miss Joan. It really was every bit as good as you said."

She accepted her due. "Of course it was. You don't stay in business as long as I have by lying to people. Don't let Rae work you too hard," she told him as an afterthought as Seamus's great-nephew began to leave the diner.

Sully's mouth curved a little as he took in her warning. "Not possible," he replied just before he took his leave.

The twenty-some-odd mile trip to the J-H Ranch went by so quickly, Sully found that he was there before he realized it. If it weren't for the tall wooden gate proclaiming the ranch's name, he wouldn't even have known that he had reached his destination. He would have just thought he was out on the open range.

Part of the problem was that the land had a sameness to it that didn't set apart one area from another.

Getting out of the 4x4 truck he had rented at the airport when he had landed here in Texas, Sully opened the gate. Getting back in, he drove through to the other side, then got out a second time in order to close the gate behind him. He didn't want to accidentally allow one of the horses to escape, although right now, he saw no sign of any kind of life forms in the vicinity.

Well, you said you wanted a change, right? Sully asked himself. *And this is certainly a change.*

While Aurora wasn't a bustling metropolis the

way Los Angeles and San Francisco were, it was definitely not anywhere nearly as deserted-looking and desolate as the land just outside of Forever was.

A person really had to be comfortable in their own skin to live out here, Sully thought. Otherwise, they could easily go stir-crazy inside of a day and a half.

Maybe two if they were particularly well-adjusted, he mused.

For a moment, he seriously considered turning the truck around, returning to the airport and catching a flight back to civilization.

The moment passed.

He was here, he silently argued, and Seamus seemed to think that being here would help him get through this unsettled part of his existence. He might as well at least meet this ranch foreman who was going to put him to work the second he set foot on the property.

He glanced at Miss Joan's map that he had placed on the passenger seat in the truck. It looked as if the ranch house was straight ahead—wherever that was.

Sully drove more than a mile beyond the gate before he finally caught sight of the ranch house. There looked to be another structure some distance behind it. He guessed it was either the barn or the stable.

He still didn't have all these ranching terms straight, he thought and wondered if Miss Joan's foreman would cut him some slack until he got oriented. He hoped the man didn't turn out to be one of these smug characters that built up his ego on the carcasses of workers he put down.

"Can't worry about that," Sully muttered. He was here, and he had to make the most of it. He hadn't traveled all this way looking to make new friends. He just wanted to get back his zest for life. The zest he'd lost along the way while tracking down a serial killer.

Sully decided that he might as well pull his vehicle up in front of the ranch house and see if there was anyone there who could tell him where he could find the ranch foreman. He didn't want to wander around aimlessly—for all he knew, that could get him shot out here.

Sully smiled grimly. He supposed that would be one way to deal with the funk he had slipped into.

After parking the truck, he got out of the cab. For now he left the one suitcase he'd packed where he'd put it, in the back seat. No sense in lugging it around until he found the foreman.

Sully smiled to himself as he approached the ranch house. The outside looked as if it had come straight out of one of those old Westerns he used to watch with his father. According to his dad, Angus, the Westerns had been old when he was a kid watching them with his father. That just made them classics in his book, his father had said.

Smiling to himself as he recalled the old memory, Sully knocked on the door.

When there was no answer, he knocked again. And again after he'd let a couple of minutes pass.

After the fourth time, he decided that no one was home and he was going to have to search for this elusive ranch foreman somewhere else.

Sully looked around. Maybe the man was in the large structure located some distance behind the house. It was worth a shot.

Sully had just turned away and gone down the three steps off the front porch when the front door suddenly opened.

Finally! Sully thought turning back around.

The single celebratory word faded instantly as the person he found himself looking up at turned out not to be the foreman.

It wasn't a man at all.

Instead, it was a slender young woman who appeared to be in her twenties. She had long straight black hair pulled back into a ponytail, prominent cheekbones and the most incredible blue eyes he had ever seen.

For a moment, the blue eyes held him captive, melting time and space into a single entity.

It took concentrated effort for him to finally come back to his senses.

"Yes?" One hand on her hip, the woman fired the single word at him like a bullet. Rather than friendly, she seemed exasperated.

Sully found himself wondering why. "Um, Miss Joan sent me."

"Of course she did," the slender young woman in jeans and a work shirt said with a sigh, looking more harassed. "You got any gear?"

He hadn't the slightest idea what she was talking about. "Gear?"

Her impatient look grew only more so.

"Things," she told him. "Your possessions, clothes, whatever."

He felt like an idiot, but then, people didn't talk the way she did back home. And they didn't snap their questions unless they were interrogating someone.

"Oh, in the truck," he said, then to make sure he was being clear, he jerked a thumb in the direction of the vehicle parked close by.

The woman's expression looked no friendlier. "You can park your car behind the house and your gear in the bunkhouse."

"Bunkhouse?"

"Behind the stable," she said. Since it was obvious that didn't clear anything up, she said, "C'mon, I'll show you." In a second, she was down the steps and striding toward the rear of the house ahead of him.

They were not starting off on the right foot, Sully thought. Hell, he'd encountered friendlier criminals. Raising his voice, he called after her. "Wait!"

The woman swung around on her heel, still looking as if her supply of patience was seriously depleting by the second. She didn't say anything, but her entire countenance let him know that she was waiting for him to say something.

Obviously, conversation was not at a premium around here.

"I'm looking for the foreman," he told her. Since she was still standing where she'd stopped, he crossed to her. "Ray Mulcahy."

She continued looking at him as if waiting for

something to dawn on him. When it didn't, she said, "You found her."

"Where?" he asked, looking around. And then the pronoun she'd used suddenly echoed in his brain. "Her?" he asked incredulously.

She opened her mouth, and he had a feeling she was about to say something less than flattering, but then she closed it again. Regrouping, the woman said, "You're serious."

"Yes."

Blowing out a breath, she spread her hands wide and said, "Here."

Sully stared at the shapely woman, dumbfounded. So much for the sanctity of old Westerns. "*You're* the foreman?" he questioned in disbelief.

It wasn't the first time one of the down-on-his-luck drifters Miss Joan had decided to take in looked appalled at the idea of having a woman giving him orders.

"I am. Something wrong with that?" Rae asked.

"No, no," Sully denied, trying not to trip over his own tongue.

He had grown up in a house of capable females. He had no problem with the idea of a woman running the ranch and issuing orders—he just really wished he'd been briefed about that ahead of time so he wouldn't have come across like a dolt.

Belatedly, he said, "I'm fine with that."

Rae took a deep breath, silently telling herself not to get on her soapbox. Scrutinizing the man in front of her, she decided that he didn't really look as if the idea of having a woman telling him what to do went against his grain. But the guy did look stunned.

She came to the only conclusion she could. "Miss Joan didn't tell you, did she?"

Sully allowed himself a hint of a smile. "That she did not." Then, because he could be seen as partially to blame, he said, "In all fairness, I didn't ask. She just said to go find the foreman, Ray Mulcahy."

And therein lay the problem, Rae thought. "Rae's short for Rachel," she told him.

"Oh. Never thought of that," he confessed.

And then, for the first time in a while, Sully started to laugh.

Rae's eyes narrowed, and she felt her back going up again. She'd worked hard to get and keep this position. Miss Joan was charitable, but the woman was also tough and gave nothing away that hadn't been earned.

"What's so funny?" she asked.

It took Sully a second to catch his breath. "My sisters are really going to get a kick out of this when I tell them about how I put my foot in my mouth."

"You have sisters?" she asked.

The drifters who came through professed to be loners and kept to themselves for the most part. They hardly ever volunteered any details about themselves, and certainly never this soon.

Maybe this one wasn't just a drifter, she thought.

"And brothers," Sully told her.

Somehow, it felt comforting to mention his family. That surprised him, because all he'd wanted to do in the last few weeks was just detach himself from everyone and everything.

"And a whole bunch of cousins," he added, "almost half of whom are female." He offered her an apologetic smile. "Sorry, I didn't mean to sound like I was insulting you before."

"You weren't," Rae replied.

Even if he had, it wasn't the sort of thing she admitted. To do so would have been to expose her own feelings, and she never did that.

Rae examined him more closely. He had a tired look about him, she decided. But he didn't appear as if he'd been knocked down one too many times or lost one con too many. That raised questions for her.

"Why are you here again?" Rae asked.

He wondered if she was trying to trip him up. "Miss Joan sent me."

"To work?" she questioned.

Sully thought for a second, wanting to get the wording just right. "She said something about earning my keep."

Rae studied the man next to her, trying to work this out in her head. He didn't look like a wrangler, but then, neither did Rawlings or Warren, the men who were currently working on the ranch.

But there was something different about him, something she couldn't quite put her finger on. She didn't like not knowing. Not knowing made her feel as if she wasn't fully prepared for whatever might come down the road.

"Where are you from?" she asked.

"Aurora. California," Sully added when the young woman who was Miss Joan's unlikely foreman continued looking at him blankly.

"California," she repeated. "And you worked your way here?"

"I flew," Sully told her, not really sure just what the woman was asking him.

This was still not really making any sense to Rae. "To Forever?" she asked skeptically.

Sully still didn't see what the problem seemed to be. "Yes."

Rae's eyebrows drew together over penetrating blue eyes. "On purpose?"

He nearly laughed at the disbelieving expression on her face but instinctively knew that would not go over too well with this woman.

So instead, he told her, "Seamus, my great-uncle, thought I might like it here."

"This great-uncle of yours, Uncle Seamus," she said, wrapping her tongue around the man's name. "He doesn't like you very much, does he?"

The way she said it, it wasn't a question—it was a conclusion.

Chapter 3

Sully looked at the woman, wondering if Rae was trying to goad him or if this was actually her opinion. He couldn't help wondering what Seamus would have thought of this feisty five-four embodiment of womanhood.

He probably would have liked her, Sully decided. His great-uncle liked women with fire in their blood who weren't afraid to speak their mind.

"Never had a reason to believe that before," Sully finally replied.

Rae shrugged, her shoulders moving carelessly beneath her checked work shirt.

"Have it your way. Anyway, you're in luck," she told him. "Early this morning I found a whole length of fence that needs to be replaced and you look more able-bodied, like you could probably do a better job of it than the two wranglers I've got here working on the ranch now."

Leading the way to her truck so she could drive him over to the location, Rae stopped walking for a moment. She decided it would be more prudent for her to ask rather than just to assume. "You do know how to dig post holes and swing a sledgehammer, don't you?"

There was a fifty-fifty chance she wasn't trying to insult him, Sully thought. In either case, he answered, "I think I can manage."

Rae nodded. She'd thought as much. "Good. At any rate, you probably can't be any worse at it than Rawlings and Warren are."

"Rawlings and Warren?" he echoed. He was trying to keep all the names straight, having a feeling that Rae Mulcahy wasn't much for repetition.

Rae nodded. "Those are the current two drifters that Miss Joan okayed to work on the ranch. Actually," she reflected, "Mr. Harry was the one who gave the okay in this case."

"Mr. Harry, that would be Miss Joan's husband?" Sully asked.

He was fairly certain that Miss Joan's husband and Mr. Harry were the same person, but he didn't want to take anything for granted and make a mistake. He had a feeling that people around here were pretty touchy. He wasn't really familiar with the names and dynamics of this hamlet yet, and he didn't want to step on any toes if he could help it.

This time Rae didn't stop walking as she spared him a quick glance. "Is that just a lucky guess on your part or are you bucking for sharpest tool in the tool box?" she asked.

He got the feeling that he was attempting to maneuver across a chasm walking on a tightrope and trying not to lose his balance—while his foreman was rooting for the rope.

"Why don't we split the difference and just move on?" Sully suggested diplomatically.

"Get in," she told him, indicating the truck. When she got in behind the steering wheel, she waited for him to sit down on his side before she asked, "What's your name, anyway?" Rae had suddenly realized that while this new man knew her name, she hadn't bothered finding out his.

"Sully," he answered just as she started up the truck.

Rae frowned, obviously rolling the name over in her head. "What kind of a name is Sully for a man?" she asked.

"What kind of name is Ray for a woman?" he countered.

"It's Rachel," she reminded him pointedly. "But men don't seem to be able to take orders very well from a Rachel out here. They will, though, take orders from someone named Rae."

Sully nodded. "Point taken. And it's Sullivan," he told her after a beat. "My full name," he added when she made no response.

She ran the name through her mind. "Sully's faster to say."

"That's what I thought."

"You got a last name, Sully?" she asked, sparing him a glance now that they were out in completely open country. "Or is that it?"

"Cavanaugh," Sully told her. "My last name's Cavanaugh."

"Sullivan Cavanaugh," Rae repeated. He wasn't sure if she was mocking him or trying it on for size. "That's quite a mouthful. Anyway, when you get a chance, you can store your gear in there," she told him, indicating the single-story structure they were passing at the moment. "You can sleep in there at the end of the day, too."

The structure wasn't very much to look at, he thought as they made their way to the open range. "Was that the bunkhouse?"

"You guessed it. It's closer than the hotel," she told him drily. "I'll introduce you to Rawlings and Warren—they should be working on the fencing by now—and then you can get started. Dinner's at six—unless the job runs over. It's served in the main house," she told him, then in case he wondered about the logistics, she explained, "There's no kitchen in the bunkhouse."

He figured as much. "Understood.

"You got work gloves?" she asked as the question suddenly occurred to her.

"No." He'd noticed a general store in town. He could always get a pair there.

Rae frowned slightly.

"It figures." And, even though she was driving, she paused to take a closer look at his hands. Taking one of his hands in hers, she gave it a cursory glance. "No gloves," she repeated. "Your hands are softer than Miss Joan's. Let me guess, you've never done any physical labor before."

"I have," Sully contradicted. He didn't care for the woman's way of passing quick judgments. "I just didn't think to bring any gloves when I packed."

"Left in a hurry?" she asked. It was a rhetorical question she didn't expect him to answer. "Well, we'll see if we can find you a pair. Wouldn't want you to mess up those soft hands of yours any more than you really have to."

Foreman or not, he had had just about enough of the woman's goading attitude. "Just show me the area that you want me to fix and I'll worry about my hands."

She drove to a section of the fence that was clearly in disrepair. It appeared to be about a hairbreadth away from falling over.

Sully noticed the frown on her face was growing more pronounced the closer they came to their destination.

"Something wrong?" he finally asked the woman.

"Yes, there's something wrong," she snapped, although this time it didn't sound as if her annoyance was directed at him or his question. "There should be two people over here."

She pulled up abruptly, parking the truck. Getting out, she got up into the back of the flatbed and then turned 360 degrees around, trying to get a wider view.

It didn't help.

Rae started to climb down from the flatbed and was surprised when Sully suddenly offered her his hand.

At first she started to ignore it, then, blowing out a huff of angry air, she wrapped her hand around his and got down.

"Thanks." Begrudgingly, she all but bit off the word.

He wondered if she had always been this angry, or if it was something she had developed working out here. Either way, he wondered what she looked like when she smiled.

"I take it your two wranglers are supposed to be here," he surmised.

"They're not *my* wranglers," she corrected. "And yes, they're supposed to be here. They're supposed to be working to fix the damn fence." She let out an exasperated huff. "I had a bad feeling about those two from the minute each of them first set foot on the ranch. Mr. Harry just got too big a heart."

Having said that, the foreman looked at Sully accusingly.

"I wouldn't know anything about that," he said by way of denial. "I only met Miss Joan, and she didn't really strike me as a pushover."

"That's because she's not—that doesn't mean she

doesn't have a good heart," Rae quickly interjected in case he was going to comment on that.

"Never said she didn't," Sully replied.

Standing next to the truck, she looked around again. There was still no sign of either one of the two men who were supposedly currently involved in earning their keep on the ranch.

This was going to put fixing the fence seriously behind schedule, Rae thought irritably.

"Well, those two had better show up if they know what's good for them. In the meantime, I need you to get to work before this whole fence falls down." She paused, assessing the man before her. "You want me to show you what to do?"

Amusement curved his lips. He resisted the temptation to tell her to go ahead and demonstrate. "I think I can handle it."

"For all our sakes, I hope so," she told him. "I'm going to take the truck and go back to the bunkhouse." Surveying the work that had to be done, she wasn't sure if she was making a mistake. "You sure you'll be all right if I leave you here?"

"Yeah." As she started to get back in behind the steering wheel, Sully told her almost conversationally, "But if you happen to see buzzards circling this area, I'd take it as a personal favor if you came back."

Rae looked at him. "By then it'll probably be too late," she answered matter-of-factly.

The next moment, the sound of the truck's engine starting up pierced the otherwise quiet atmosphere. Two minutes later, she was gone.

Sully looked at the posts that were lined up on the ground beside carefully cut lengths of lumber, a sledgehammer, a shovel and what appeared to be enough boxes of nails to build a small city.

It looked as if he had everything he needed, he thought. Time to earn his keep. Sully picked up the shovel and got started.

This work was hotter than he'd thought it would be. Sully held out as long as he could, but when rivulets of sweat all but sealed his shirt to his body, he peeled the shirt off and then continued working on the fence bare-chested.

That was the way Rae found him when she returned a little while later.

Her breath involuntarily caught in her throat as she absorbed the sight: the stranger's body glistening with perspiration, the muscles in his upper arms straining with each movement he made. The man had abdominal muscles that looked as if they had been chiseled out of rock, and for the first time since she was fifteen years old, Rae's mind suddenly went numb.

The next moment, because there was someone else in the truck with her, she managed to slowly regulate her breathing and collect herself.

"Who's that?" Jack Rawlings, the passenger in the truck, asked.

"Someone who's not afraid of work," she replied, taking no pains to hide her displeasure with her passenger.

Getting out of the truck, she strode up behind Sully. "Maybe you should put that shirt back on, Cavanaugh," she told him.

Caught off guard, Sully swung around. He looked at Rae and then at the man with her. "You have a dress code out here?" he asked the woman, keeping an innocent expression on his face.

"No, other than making sure you keep your pants on," she informed him. "But that sun is pretty merciless around this time of day. If you don't put your shirt back on, you're probably going to watch your skin start peeling off before evening."

He shrugged off her so-called concern. "Don't worry about it. I'm pretty resilient." Sully looked around the foreman's shoulder at the man standing just behind her, taking all this. He made an assumption. "I thought you said there were two other men working on the ranch."

"There were. There are," Rae said, correcting herself. "But apparently the other one—Warren—decided to take off, at least according to Rawlings here."

"He did," the other man, a rather dusty, jowly-looking man who appeared to be somewhere in his late forties, said. The years hadn't been kind to him, and he looked as if he knew it and resented the fact. "When I woke up this morning, he was gone."

Taking a time-out, Sully leaned against his shovel. "Are his clothes gone?"

Jack Rawlings looked at him blankly. "What?"

"Warren's clothes," Sully repeated. "Are they gone, too?"

The man looked irritated. "I dunno. I guess so," he mumbled. And then he seemed to take offense. "Hey, I don't go looking through a man's things," he protested, looking at Rae rather than this offensive newcomer. "That's private."

"You're right," Sully agreed. "I just meant that if this missing wrangler didn't take his things with him, maybe he's not really missing. Maybe he's just somewhere else on the ranch." He directed his conversation to Rae. "It's a big ranch."

That was all relative, Rae thought. "Not compared to the other ranches around here."

He wasn't familiar with the area, but he supposed that she would know better than he did. But that didn't change his initial assumption.

"Still, a man could go somewhere and not be seen." His eyes swept over the wrangler Rae had brought back with her, and then returned to Rae. "You've got several structures from what I can see, not to mention all this wide-open acreage. Could this Warren be on another part of the ranch, doing something you assigned him to do?" Sully asked.

Rather than answer him, Rae turned her eyes on Rawlings. The wrangler raised his shoulders in complete frustration. "I don't know. Maybe. All I know is he wasn't there when I woke up and he didn't leave me no note to tell me where he was at. Not that he would," the wrangler added in what Sully took to be disgust.

"Maybe someone should look around for him be-
fore deciding that the man just took off for good,"
Sully suggested to Rae, picking up his shovel again.
"But that's just my opinion."

"And a pretty good one. You heard the man," Rae
said, turning toward the wrangler. "Start looking."

"What, he's my new boss now?" Rawlings asked
resentfully, jerking his thumb at Sully and looking
disgruntled.

"No, but I am, and I just gave you a direct order,"
Rae pointed out, looking at Rawlings expectantly.

"That's going to take me forever on foot," Rawlings protested.

Rae took off a key from her key ring and then
held it out to the wrangler. "Go back and get the
other truck. And try not to drive it into a ditch," she
warned. "It belongs to Miss Joan."

"What she gonna do if something happens to it?"
Rawlings asked sarcastically.

"Trust me," Rae answered, looking up into his
eyes. "You do *not* want to find out."

Rawlings frowned as he took the key from her.
"I'll be careful."

"Wise decision," she told him.

Taking the key and putting it into his pocket, Rawlings started to go off in the direction of the bunkhouse. Just before he left, the wrangler glanced over
his shoulder and glared at the newcomer. When Sully
glanced his way, Rawlings ducked down his head
and quickened his pace.

"I don't think I made any points with your man,"

Sully told her as he got back to digging holes for the posts.

Although she didn't want to, Rae found herself staring at the way the man's muscles strained and seemed to bulge with every movement he made with the shovel. It took considerable effort to draw her eyes away.

She replayed what he had asked earlier when Rawlings had told her that the other man had taken off. It raised questions in her mind.

"What did you say you did before you came here?" she asked.

"I didn't say." Pausing for a second, he spared her a glance. "You didn't ask," he reminded her in case Rae thought he was being flippant.

"I'm asking now," she told him, waiting.

"A little of this, a little of that," he said vaguely.

Some people reacted strangely when they found out that he was a detective with the Aurora police department, so it wasn't the first thing he volunteered when he was asked.

"Do this and that have a name?" Rae asked him pointedly.

"Yes," he answered, his breath growing a little short as he dug yet another hole. He was grateful that there were only two more holes left to dig.

"So are you going to tell me what you did, or are you waiting for me to say 'pretty please?'" Rae asked. When she saw his mouth curve in a deep smile, she decided she'd had enough of playing games. "What the hell were you?"

"A detective," Sully answered. Crossing his arms and resting them on top of the shovel handle, he added, "I still am."

Chapter 4

Rae looked at the man who was working up another sweat before her with renewed interest. "A detective?"

Because of what he was doing, it took Sully a second before he could answer. "Yes."

She tried to reconcile the image of the man before her with the one he'd just told her about.

"You're one of those people other people hire to find someone?" she questioned.

"No," he explained patiently as he continued digging the last post hole. The ground around here felt as if it was made out of clay. Hard clay. Trying to dig a hole in it was both a challenge and at times felt like exercise in futility.

With every move he made, he could feel the muscles in his arms vigorously protesting. "I'm one of those people who works for the police department," he answered.

That made even less sense to her than her first assumption. "You work for the police department," she repeated.

"That's...what... I...said."

Maybe he was in worse shape than he thought, Sully decided. Digging shouldn't be taking this kind of a toll on him. He stopped for a minute longer to catch his breath and then resumed digging.

Rae moved around so that she was directly in front of this so-called police detective in wrangler's clothing. "If you're telling the truth—"

He stopped dueling with the cement-like soil to look at her. At this point, he was up for only one battle at a time. It was either digging or matching wits with this foreman.

"Why would I lie about that?" Sully asked.

"Okay," she amended. "You're a police detective." She granted him that, although part of her was still dubious. "What the hell are you doing out here?"

He looked accusingly at the shovel and then decided maybe he was better off digging. With luck, Rae would get tired of this and leave him to do the work.

"Right now, trying to dig a hole in this soil and wondering what the hell is in it to make it almost completely impenetrable," he answered.

Rae frowned, waving away his response. She could see what he was doing, and that wasn't what she meant. "Sections out here in this area are really hard to dig in, but that's not the point right now." Taking hold of the handle of his shovel, she held it fast so he was forced to stop digging altogether—not that he minded all that much. "What are you doing here, Cavanaugh?" she repeated with more feeling. It didn't make any sense to her, and she hated things that didn't make sense. "Forever isn't exactly on the map as a prime vacation spot."

"I'm not out here on a vacation," Sully informed her. "I'm out here to clear my head."

"You said you were from California. There have *got* to be places you could do that in that are closer to home," Rae pointed out.

His eyes met hers. She continued looking at him, waiting for an answer. The woman was pushy, he'd give her that. She was also getting on his nerves.

"Maybe I don't want to be closer to home," he countered. "Now, if you're through interrogating me, I'd like to get back to work."

That wasn't entirely true, he thought, but it was better than butting heads with this woman.

But Rae refused to back off. "*Why* don't you want to be closer to home? What happened?"

If she still had a home—and a family—nothing would have made her leave. She would have fought to stay. She couldn't understand someone willingly abandoning his home.

Okay, he'd been polite enough. Time to mark his territory, Sully thought. "That, Ms. Mulcahy, is none of your business. It has nothing to do with how well I work or how fast I can get things you need done."

Annoyed, Rae decided to back off for the time being. She could be patient. She'd get the information she wanted another way.

"Prickly sort, aren't you?" she commented. "All right, I'll leave you to it, then. And when you finish digging that hole, start putting the poles up. I'll be back later."

"Looking forward to it," Sully told her. There was no emotion in his voice to give her any indication how he actually meant that.

Rae opened her mouth to make a retort, then decided there was no point. Instead she got into her truck without another word and drove back to the bunkhouse.

After considerable effort, Sully finished digging the last hole. Taking a five-minute break, he next turned his attention to properly sinking the new posts into the holes he had dug.

He quickly discovered that doing that on his own was a lot more challenging than he'd initially thought. The problem arose because the object was to make sure that the post was straight once the dirt was firmly packed around it.

After two failures, he tried a third time.

Sully once again leaned the pole against his shoulder as he grappled with refilling the hole. He had finally gotten the first pole in position when he heard the sound of a truck approaching.

He blew out a breath, not sure if he was relieved or annoyed at the interruption.

"Looks like the boss lady's checking up on me," he muttered under his breath.

He would have preferred getting at least one— if not more—of the poles up before Mulcahy came back, but obviously there was nothing he could do about it now, Sully thought.

However, when the truck pulled up next to him, it wasn't Rae who got out of the cab. Instead, it was the man she had introduced as Jack Rawlings and another, taller man who got out on the driver's side.

Pausing, Sully dragged the back of his wrist across his forehead in an effort to wipe away the sweat before it dripped into his eyes and stung.

He did a quick assessment of the man next to Rawlings. He was about half a head taller than Rawlings, but he looked even more out of shape. Soft and pudgy-looking—in Sully's estimation the so-called wrangler appeared as if he would have been more at home behind a desk.

"I take it you're the missing wrangler," Sully said to Rawlings's companion.

"Missing?" the man repeated, confused. When he squinted, looking from Sully to Rawlings, his eyes all but disappeared. "I wasn't missing. I just had something to do, that's all." He glanced again at the man beside him, clearly annoyed and yet somewhat afraid of showing it. "You told this guy I was missing?"

It was apparent that Rawlings didn't do well with

blame. "You weren't in your bunk when I woke up. How'm I supposed to know you didn't take off?"

"The last time I looked, you weren't my ex-wife," John Warren all but snapped. He backtracked a little as he added, "I don't have to ask your permission to go somewhere."

In Sully's estimation, this could turn ugly given enough fuel. He didn't want to get caught up in the middle of that.

"Hey, guys, I could use a hand here," Sully said, calling the wranglers' attention to the pole that was still propped up against his shoulder. "If one of you could just hold this upright and straight, the job would go a lot faster."

It was plain by the look on Rawlings's face that everything was going to rub the man the wrong way no matter what was said. "You her junior foreman now?" Rawlings challenged belligerently.

"I'm just trying to get the job done," Sully answered. Thinking that being nice to the wrangler wasn't working, he had nothing to lose by putting Rawlings in his place. "Maybe if you put down that giant chip on your shoulder, you could move a little faster."

Rawlings looked incensed, and for a split second, it seemed as if the wrangler was going to launch himself right at him, Sully thought.

But obviously at the last moment, common sense—and the fact that Sully was close to a foot taller than he was—prevailed.

Rawlings frowned, glaring at Sully. "This isn't over, you know," he warned.

"Didn't think it was," Sully replied mildly. It took effort, but he forced himself to get back to the immediate problem he was dealing with. "Now can one of you hold this?"

It was obvious that Rawlings wasn't about to make an effort, so Warren stepped up. "I'll do it," the no-longer-missing man volunteered.

"Thanks," Sully said.

When Warren wrapped his arms around the post, Sully picked up the discarded shovel. Within moments, he was attempting to evenly shovel dirt around the pole. Although this job was a lot less taxing than digging the holes had been, Sully could swear he felt calluses forming on the palms of his hands.

"Hey," Warren called over to the man who had supposedly gone looking for him. When Rawlings, who had just sunk down on the ground some distance away from them, looked in their direction, Warren told him, "We could use some help over here."

But Rawlings didn't budge. "Looks like you've got it all under control to me."

"Then maybe you should get your eyes checked," Sully told the inert man in an even voice, one that gave every indication that he expected to be listened to.

He wasn't here to win any popularity contest, Sully thought. Right now, he just wanted to get a job done, one that Miss Joan's foreman had assigned to him. He had no idea what Rawlings's problem was, but he wasn't about to let it get in the way of their getting this job done.

"Now get over here and help Warren hold this pole in place so that it looks straight and I can get it put into the ground properly."

"C'mon, Rawlings," Warren appealed to the other wrangler. "The sooner you help, the sooner we'll get all these posts in the ground so we can all get back to the bunkhouse."

Again Rawlings wasn't about to take the blame. "Hey, I'm not the one who took off," he snapped.

"You're also not the one who did any work today," Sully reminded the antagonistic wrangler. His voice was low and civilized. But there was no mistaking that the man behind the calm voice could only be pushed so far and no more.

Swearing and muttering some unintelligible things under his breath, Rawlings joined them and grudgingly put his back into it.

After she'd made sure that both Rawlings and the "missing" Warren were on their way to help Cavanaugh, Rae made a beeline for town and Miss Joan's diner. She had questions that needed answering, and it seemed that she was only going to get those answers from one source.

The moment she walked into the diner, she saw the person she needed to talk to.

"Miss Joan, about that new guy you just sent me,"

Rae said as she crossed to the counter that ran along the back of the diner.

Miss Joan had just served one of her regular customers. She looked up the moment she heard her name. Despite the fact that she recognized the young woman's voice, Miss Joan was still surprised to see Rae at the diner.

Collecting herself, she assumed a dour expression as she asked, "What happened to 'hello'?"

"Hello," Rae said with just a touch of impatience before she got back to her question. This time she phrased it differently. "What's that's guy's story?"

"What do you mean?" Miss Joan asked. Innocence did not look at home on the woman. The best she could do was display a poker face.

Rae had a feeling that Miss Joan knew exactly what she meant, but she answered the question anyway. "He said he's a police detective."

Miss Joan nodded. "That's what I heard, yes," she confirmed.

Rae pressed her lips together. She was accustomed to having down-on-their-luck cowboys or wannabe cowboys working on the ranch as well as other men whose previous vocations were usually of the nondescript variety.

The one thing the men all had in common was that they were just passing through Forever and the J-H Ranch because life had ridden roughshod over them.

But even so, there appeared to be something rather different about this latest man who had popped up at the ranch.

He wasn't like the others.

Miss Joan indicated the counter stool with her eyes, but Rae felt too wired to sit down.

"Why would a police detective be out here?" Rae asked.

"Maybe he just needed a little peace of mind," Miss Joan suggested. "Police detectives are people, too, you know, Rae."

"I know that." She closed her eyes for a moment, as if to gather strength. "Are you sure he really is a police detective? Did someone vouch for him?"

"Yes," Miss Joan answered simply.

She wasn't prepared to have Rae challenge her statement. "Who?"

Miss Joan looked at her in stony silence for a moment before finally answering. "The best person I know outside of Harry," Miss Joan assured her. "Why? Is there something about him that's bothering you?"

Rae shook her head. "He's not the usual type who works on the ranch."

"As I recall, neither were you at first when I decided to put you in charge of the J-H," Miss Joan reminded her foreman. "More than one person told me not to do it."

"That's different," Rae protested. "You *knew* me."

Miss Joan raised her eyes to Rae's. "I didn't put you in charge because I knew you. I did it because I had a gut feeling that you could do the job and that being in charge at the ranch was what you needed in your life to finally get you on the right track."

Rae wanted to argue with the woman, to insist again that it wasn't the same thing. But Miss Joan had an aura about her that transcended logic, and she knew that almost better than anyone. When her father had died, leaving her alone, and she had felt so lost, so hopeless that she just couldn't go on, it was Miss Joan who had been her lifeline. Miss Joan who had bullied her into not giving up and continuing to live.

Maybe, in her own way, she was doing the same thing for this man, this police detective she had sent to her to work with.

"And you have a gut feeling about this Sully?" Rae asked.

"Let's just say he's not anyone that I'm going to be worried about when it comes to working out. Now, if you have a problem with him," Miss Joan continued, looking at Rae intently, "I suggest you talk it out with him. Best way to resolve things," she told the girl she had taken in and watched blossom over the years. She eyed Rae for a moment when the latter made no comment. "We okay?"

"Yes, Miss Joan," Rae replied dutifully. To try to go against the woman's wishes would just be ungrateful.

"All right then." Miss Joan took out a pie that was in the display case and placed it on the counter. "Why don't you take a piece of one of Angel's pies with you and get back to overseeing the ranch while I get back to doing my job?" she suggested, slicing a piece of the peach cobbler on the counter and placing it into a small white container. Snapping the lid into place, she pushed the container toward Rae.

Rae picked up the container and smiled her thanks at the woman. "I'll have this after dinner."

"Warm it up. It'll taste better that way. You might also think about sharing it," Miss Joan added. "I cut a big enough piece for that."

Rae looked down at the container in her hand. She didn't have to ask Miss Joan whom she wanted her to share the piece of pie with. That was silently implied.

"Maybe I'll do that," Rae answered, not wanting to commit herself to anything one way or another.

Turning on her heel, she made her way out of the semi-filled diner.

Just who was this new man to Miss Joan? Was he a relative? A relative of a person who had once figured prominently in Miss Joan's life? Miss Joan had said that the person who had vouched for Sully was someone she considered to be the most decent man she knew after her husband.

Rae frowned to herself as she got into her truck. She tucked the container on the floor beneath the passenger seat.

Her conversation with Miss Joan had raised more questions for her than answers. The one thing she was certain of was that she was going to approach this police detective with caution as she continued to assess the situation. She was determined to find an answer as to what someone like that was doing digging holes and putting up posts on a small, run-of-the-mill ranch instead of taking a vacation at some showy resort or, at the very least, some trendy beach in his home state.

Something had made that man come out here, and she intended to find out what.

Chapter 5

"Is now a bad time?"

Startled, Rae turned away from what she was doing to see Miss Joan's husband standing in the kitchen doorway, peering in.

"I knocked," the mild-looking man explained politely, "but there was no answer, so I just let myself in. I hope you don't mind."

Harry Monroe remained where he was in the doorway, waiting for a sign from the young woman that he could enter.

Rae quickly wiped her hands on the dish towel that she kept slung over the back of a nearby chair and immediately crossed the floor to the man who was the closest thing she had to a grandfather. Harry Monroe just exuded kindliness.

"This is your ranch house, Mr. Harry. You have absolutely every right to come in," Rae told the man, although she had to admit that she was surprised to see him. Miss Joan's husband didn't normally come out to the ranch without calling ahead first.

"Still, if you're busy, I can come back," he offered gently, pointing toward the outer door for emphasis.

Rae laughed at that. "We're *always* busy here, sir. But right now, I'm just putting our dinner on the table." She gestured toward the table settings she had just finished putting out. Dinner had arrived, fully prepared, half an hour ago. Everything else had been stacked up in their oversize refrigerator. "Rosa's a fantastic cook," she interjected, referring to one of the young women Miss Joan currently had working at the diner, who had delivered the boxed-up meal. "She's almost as good as Angel."

The man nodded in agreement, although it would have been a surprise to hear him disagree. No one in town could ever remember the man having anything bad to say about anyone.

"That she is," Harry said, then added, "If you'd like, Miss Joan can tell her to perhaps come out to the ranch during the week, prepare the meals here."

But Rae shook her head. "No, that's not necessary. I'm just happy that Rosa stocks up the refrigerator when she comes." The woman always left a week's worth of prepared meals, not just for her but for the wranglers, as well. She didn't know what she would have done without Rosa's help. "I don't like to cook very much," she admitted.

"You do more than enough out here already," Harry assured her. "Trust me, Miss Joan and I wouldn't want to be responsible for killing the goose that lays the golden eggs."

While Rae liked being appreciated, compliments always made her feel uncomfortable, as if she didn't know where to look or what to say.

"You asked if this was a bad time," she reminded the man. "Is this about that police detective Miss Joan sent to stay here?"

Harry smiled at the way she'd phrased her question. "So you've discovered his background, have you?" the man surmised.

She didn't know if Harry thought it best if that remained a secret, but since she'd said it, she couldn't very well take it back.

"The topic came up," Rae answered evasively.

"So how's he working out?" Harry asked her, his tone friendly as always.

Rae decided that it was best just to remain factual. "Well, unlike the last two who came here, this one doesn't seem to have an aversion to work. Or to getting dirty," she added, thinking of the way Sully had looked earlier today the first time she'd checked on him. "As a matter of fact, from what I saw, he was doing a pretty good job putting up fence posts." She kept her praise down to a reasonable level, not wanting Miss Joan's husband to get the wrong idea. "And as you know, this isn't the easiest dirt to dig in."

Mr. Harry laughed like a man who could attest

to that firsthand. "Amen to that," he answered. "So you got him settled in?"

Rae went back to setting the table. She nodded in response to the man's question.

"He didn't seem to have much, so when he finishes work for the day, he can put his stuff in the bunkhouse." She noticed the rather puzzled expression on the older man's face, but she kept on talking. "As you know, there's plenty of room there."

"The bunkhouse?" Harry repeated. Rae nodded. Looking a little embarrassed, Harry cleared his throat, then ventured an observation. "I think there's been a little miscommunication, Rachel. Miss Joan doesn't want Sully staying in the bunkhouse."

She didn't see what the problem was, or why. "That's where the wranglers always stay."

"I know, but Sully's the great-nephew of one of Miss Joan's oldest, dearest friends," he told Rae, adding, "That makes him family in her eyes."

Now it was becoming clear to her, Rae thought. She shifted uncomfortably. "And family doesn't stay in the bunkhouse," she concluded.

Harry smiled, nodding at her, apparently glad that she understood. "No," he agreed, "they don't."

"Where do you want him to stay?" she asked cautiously, watching the man's face—hoping he had some sort of alternative solution to the one that had popped up in her head.

Harry seemed oblivious to the dilemma that had just been raised.

"As I recall, this place has three bedrooms," Mr.

Harry began. When Rae made no comment, he prodded the discussion along. "Sully can sleep in one of the bedrooms that you're not using."

This was getting to be *really* uncomfortable, Rae thought, but she couldn't very well come out and say that to Mr. Harry. The ranch and the structures on it all belonged to him, and he could do anything he wanted with them as well as have whoever he wanted staying in them. She had no say in the matter.

As if reading Rae's mind, Harry said, "I know this arrangement might seem a little unusual to you, but I assure you that you don't have anything to worry about. Sully comes from an excellent family."

"So did Cain before he killed Abel," she murmured under her breath as she reached across the table to arrange the last place setting.

"But I'm definitely nothing like Cain," Sully said, walking in just behind Rae.

Rae swung around, swallowing the surprised gasp that had risen in her throat. She did what she could to smother her startled expression.

One look at Sully and it was obvious to anyone that he had been working hard for a good part of the day. There was dirt on his clothes and face, not to mention the scent of sweat coming from every inch of his body. Aside from looking exhausted, he carried himself like a man who had done more than an honest day's work.

In addition, he also looked rather satisfied with himself, Rae thought.

Harry smiled broadly at the young man. Miss

Joan had taught him not to stand on ceremony, but to seize the moment. He was still learning.

"You must be Sullivan Cavanaugh," Harry said, crossing to Sully with his hand extended.

Sully returned the smile as he took the man's hand in his and shook it.

"I guess I must be," he said by way of confirmation. "And I guess that you must be Miss Joan's husband."

Rather than look annoyed at the label, Harry's eyes crinkled as he laughed.

"That's probably going to be on my tombstone when I die," he said. "'Here lies Miss Joan's husband.'"

Rae took offense for the man, even though it appeared that Sully had meant no disrespect and Harry just took the whole thing in stride.

Glaring at Sully, she informed him, "You do realize that the only reason you're here is because Mr. Harry was kind enough to give his permission to take you in, right?"

"I'm aware of that and I appreciate it," Sully said, directing his answer toward the older gentleman. "Thank you, sir."

It was clear by Sully's demeanor that while he remained polite, Rae did *not* intimidate him the way she managed to intimidate the other two wranglers, at least whenever she reprimanded them.

Again Harry cleared his throat, as if that was a way to calm the situation down a bit.

"I didn't come here to rock any boats or rattle any

cages," he said when the two younger people looked
at him. "Those are both Miss Joan's purview," he
added with a soft, amused chuckle. "I just came to
see how you were getting along, Sully." And then he
asked formally, "Is everything to your satisfaction?"

The man was genuinely interested in his reply,
Sully realized. For a split second, Sully caught himself feeling homesick. The second passed.

"Everything is just fine," Sully replied. "They'll
be even finer once I get out of these dirty clothes
and take a shower."

"Then I won't keep you," Harry told him cheer-
fully. He looked at Rae. "Give him the room with
the bathroom," he advised.

Sully looked from Rae to the man who had just
spoken. He'd looked into the bunkhouse briefly, and
what Harry had just said didn't make any sense.

"I don't understand," Sully said. "The bunkhouse
isn't divided into rooms—unless I missed something."

Rae did her best to hide her annoyance. "What
you missed is that you're not staying in the bunkhouse," she informed Sully.

Sully stared at her. "How's that again?"

"That was my mistake," Harry said, speaking up
to take the blame and clear the air. "Rachel thought
we wanted you to stay in the bunkhouse when we
sent you over."

"And you don't?" Sully asked uncertainly.

"Miss Joan would have my head if she found out

that you were crowded in with those two other men," Harry told him, laughing at his own expense.

"I suppose she doesn't want him working, either," Rae surmised. Though she tried to suppress it, there was a less-than-happy note in her tone.

Sully didn't wait for Harry to answer. "I like to earn my keep," he informed her.

"And that's what Miss Joan likes about you, boy," Harry told him. "You don't act like you think you're entitled or privileged."

If she didn't know any better, it seemed to Rae that her boss was directing his words toward her rather than just talking to Miss Joan's unexpected guest. In either case, she resigned herself to the fact that she had her instructions.

"I guess you'd better move your things out of the bunkhouse before you take that shower," she told Sully. "Dinner'll be on the table in half an hour. If you're not here at the time, it'll be put away."

"Understood," Sully told her in a genial tone.

Harry looked pleased with what he heard. "Well, looks like everything's going well, so I'll be going now," he told Rae. "I'll let Miss Joan know that you have everything under control—as usual," the man added with a pleased smile.

Sully waited until the older man had left before he turned toward Rae. She half expected him to say something snide, because it was obvious that he had Miss Joan's blessings in this matter.

Instead, she heard him tell her, "I can stay in the bunkhouse."

She looked at him in surprise. "Why would you do that?"

In her opinion, anyone would jump at the opportunity to move into a better living situation if they had the chance. Why was Sully willing to turn it down and share his quarters with two strangers?

"I don't want you to feel uncomfortable," Sully began. "After all, you were here first."

Rae's back instantly went up. It always did whenever she thought she was being offered charity or was being looked down on. Did he think she was afraid he would try something? She could defend herself very well, thank you very much.

"Why would you think that having you staying in the main house would make me uncomfortable?" she demanded angrily.

"Then it doesn't?" Sully asked her.

She couldn't tell if he was being on the level or playing her, but she wasn't about to take a chance.

"No," Rae snapped.

"Sorry, my mistake," Sully apologized. He started to withdraw from the room. "I'll just go get my things," he told her before he left the kitchen and then the house.

Rae stood there in the kitchen, not making a move. Feeling as if she had just possibly won a battle and still somehow managed to lose the war.

The truth of it was she *didn't* want Sully staying in the house with her. She didn't want *anyone* staying in the house with her. It made her feel as if she was being hemmed in.

All in all it was rather a small house, and even though they would only be here for a minimum amount of time each day, they were bound to run into one another either in the morning or at night. Rae considered both of those times to be her private time, and she wanted to be able to just relax, not be wary of unexpectedly having contact with one of the people who were working for her.

Especially not this man.

Added to that, whether or not anyone came out and said it, this Sully character was being given preferential treatment. He *had* to be aware of that. What if he suddenly decided that he was entitled to preferential treatment from her, as well?

Or what if he wanted something from her that she had absolutely no intention of giving? She wasn't that kind of person.

Don't get ahead of yourself. Nothing's going to happen—he's got to know that Miss Joan would fillet him if he ever made a move on you she didn't approve of, great-nephew of a cherished friend or not.

With determination, Rae turned her attention to putting out that evening's dinner. Even with all of Rosa's earlier work, the meals still had to be warmed up, and at times, she had to do more than that to finish preparing the meals for them. Rae didn't mind. She viewed it as just one of her jobs, along with all the other ones she handled on the small horse ranch.

All in all, Rae had to admit that she really liked doing all the myriad things that were required of her and that went into keeping the ranch running as smoothly as it did.

Most of the time, those things involved working with the horses and putting up with the various people—men mostly—that Miss Joan and, on occasion, Mr. Harry sent out to the ranch to help with its maintenance.

Over the last few years, she had come to the conclusion that she could probably work with the devil himself if she had to—although she would have preferred not to if she had her choice, she thought with a grim smile.

However, this latest wrangler, this *police detective* Miss Joan had gifted her with, was, she had to admit, a whole different story.

She wasn't really certain how to read him or, consequently, how to react to him.

She'd concluded that he was definitely an educated man, which in itself was a pleasant change from most of the wranglers she had dealt with. And so far, he hadn't given her anything to complain about—but he hadn't even been here for twenty-four hours yet, so anything could happen.

She wasn't given to making snap decisions, Rae reminded herself as she went on putting the main course on the table and adding the two side dishes, as well. That meant she had to give the man a little time to get used to the routine here before she started finding reasons to want him to move on.

Still, she couldn't deny that there was something about the man that made her edgy. That made her

kitchen. "And you still haven't answered my question."

"*What* question?" she demanded, narrowly avoiding hitting him with a pot she was shifting from the stove to the counter.

"Do you need any help?" He nodded at what he assumed was dinner, which she appeared to have just finished heating up on the stove.

"You mean other than with getting my heart beating normally again?" she asked Sully sarcastically.

He didn't back off the way she expected him to. Instead, he seemed to take her words at their face value. "Actually," Sully told her, "if that was the case, I could help with that, too."

She left the pot of mashed potatoes where they were on top of the stove. "So aside from being a police detective, you're also a doctor on the side?"

Sully ignored the fact that her question was dripping with sarcasm and answered her as if she'd asked the question in earnest.

"No, but one of my aunts runs an ambulance service, and she insisted on teaching all of us a few basic things and what to do in life-and-death situations. I know how to give CPR," he added.

Rae spared him a quick glance before shutting off the last burner. Maybe he was on the level. Sully certainly looked sincere enough, she couldn't help thinking. For now she took his words at face value and nodded. "I'll keep that in mind."

"Good. And about my other, more mundane offer?

Helping with dinner," he prodded when she looked at him blankly.

Since it didn't look as if she was about to get him to just sit down at the table and keep out of the way, she took Sully up on his offer.

"Sure. You can carry that plate of brisket to the table."

Sully smiled in response. "I think I can manage that," he told her.

"New guy trying to make points?" Rawlings asked as he walked into what passed for a dining room but was really little more than just an extension of the kitchen.

Rae looked over toward the latest arrival and frowned. "What did I tell you about taking off your hat when you're in the house?" she asked the wrangler in a stern voice.

Rawlings scowled in response, then finally pulled the dusty Stetson off his head. "You got too many rules," he complained.

"Warren doesn't seem to think so," Rae pointed out as the other man came in to join them.

"Yeah, he just takes off without telling anyone and doesn't show up to work when he's supposed to," Rawlings told her defensively.

"Why don't we all call a truce and sit down at the table for dinner?" Sully suggested in a friendly tone. He looked from a disgruntled Rawlings to a very tired-looking Warren, who quite obviously didn't like having his faults pointed out. "It's been a long day."

"I don't need you giving us any orders, pretty boy," Rawlings growled.

"If you don't like the way things are around here, Rawlings, you can always pack up and leave," Rae informed the surly man, ladling the mashed potatoes into a serving dish. "Nobody's stopping you."

For a second, the shorter of the two wranglers glared at her belligerently. But casting a side glance at Sully, who had stopped moving and appeared to be braced for something to happen, Rawlings seemed to think better of the situation.

"Hot weather's got me on edge," he said as if that explained everything.

Rae nodded. "None of us are at our best in this kind of weather," she allowed. She was about to pick up the basket of biscuits she'd prepared and saw that Warren already had it in his hands and was headed toward the table. She inclined her head, smiling her thanks. "Thank you, Warren."

Warren looked almost sheepish to be on the receiving end of any sort of acknowledgment. "Yeah, no problem," he mumbled.

"All right, let's all sit down and eat," she told the three men around her.

There were six chairs around the table. "Does it matter where I sit?" Sully asked Rae. When she looked at him quizzically, he explained, "I just wanted to make sure that there were no designated seats. I don't want to take anyone else's chair."

"You can have that one," Rae told him, pointing to the chair that was directly opposite hers. Rawlings and Warren had already sat down in two of the other chairs.

"Who are the other two chairs for?" Sully asked, curious.

"Other people. When they're here," she added. "It all depends on how charitable Miss Joan feels like being."

"I ain't no charity case," Rawlings protested, the scowl on his face growing darker. "I work for my keep."

Rawlings appeared as if he was about to say something more in his defense, but at that point Rae raised her eyes to his face and the man grew silent. He turned his attention to his meal and chewed as if he was taking out his frustrations on the large cut of beef he had on his plate.

"This is really good," Sully told Rae, referring to the brisket. It was quite obvious that he was trying to defuse the situation before it escalated.

"I can't take the credit for it," Rae said, fending off any compliment he might follow up with.

Sully looked surprised. "I thought I saw you working over this in the kitchen."

"I was just heating it up," she told him. Unlike with Rawlings, she avoided looking up at Sully. "One of Miss Joan's girls comes by once a week to stock the refrigerator with meals she's made. It's all part of the package for working here."

"It's still really good," Sully said, trying to find a way to gracefully ease out of the conversation without giving any offense.

He had no desire to get into an argument with this woman. Miss Joan had put her in charge, and he intended to abide by that.

"Nobody's arguing that," Rae replied.

Sully smiled to himself. He had a feeling that the woman was willing to argue over just about anything she could if she felt that it rubbed her the wrong way even the slightest bit. She probably enjoyed arguing. In a way, she reminded him of his sisters.

"That's supposed to make up for the low pay," Rawlings grumbled to himself.

Rae was working hard to hang on to her temper. "Like I said, if you don't like it here, Rawlings, nobody's making you stay."

"You mean that now that *he's* here, you don't need me to stay," Rawlings retorted.

"Why don't you settle down?" Sully told the man. "That's not what she said."

It was clear that had Sully been a less able-looking man, an altercation would have broken out. But Rawlings wasn't a total hotheaded idiot, and he could see that he'd lose in any sort of a fight with the new man. So instead, he glared and went back to eating his meal in stony silence.

The rest of the meal was quiet, with all four participants observing one another and being on their respective guards.

Although silent, it was clear that Rawlings seemed ready to take offense at a moment's notice, while Warren did his best to keep his own counsel, as did Sully.

Consequently, the time it took to consume the meal seemed as if it was passing in slow motion. The minutes ticked by until finally, everyone had finished and, thanks to the two wranglers, there was nothing left of the brisket or the two side dishes.

Sully noticed that the two wranglers lost no time in clearing out and disappearing. To the bunkhouse, he imagined. Since Rae had left the table as well, he debated leaving the room himself. The silence was almost uncomfortable at this point.

But his upbringing had left some things deeply imbedded in his basic makeup.

So when Sully rose from the table, he picked up his own plate as well one of the other two plates that the two wranglers had left behind in their wake.

He walked into the kitchen proper just in time to hear Rae, her back to him, exclaim a none-too-subdued "Damn it!"

"Something wrong?"

Obviously angry, she looked at him over her shoulder. "Sneaking around again?" she accused.

"Trying to make as much noise as I can," he answered, still holding the two plates in his hands. He asked his initial question again. "Something wrong?"

"Yes, something's wrong," she retorted, waving her hand and glaring at the silent dishwasher. "The dishwasher died." From the looks of the machine, it was as old as the ranch house itself, which was over forty years old.

"You sure?" Sully asked. Sometimes these things came back to life after a good whack against one of its sides, although he wasn't about to suggest that to her.

For once, she appeared to try to contain her temper. "I don't say things just to hear myself talk," Rae informed him. "But you're welcome to try to get it to rise up from the dead if you'd like."

This was a confrontation in the making, and he knew when to back off.

"That's all right. I'm sure you know what you're talking about. Here," he offered, "I'll do the dishes—and the pots," he added, noting that there were three lined up along the sink's counter.

Rae waited for some sort of a catch. "You're volunteering to do the dishes?" she asked incredulously.

"Yeah, why?" he asked. Sully looked around, then opened the cabinet doors right beneath the sink. "Where's your dishwashing soap?" he asked. Then, bending down he spotted what he was looking for. "Oh, never mind. I found it."

For her part, Rae was still trying to process what was going on. "You don't mind doing dishes?" she asked him in disbelief.

"No. Should I?" he asked, wondering if there was some line he'd crossed or some unwritten law he'd inadvertently broken. He wasn't versed in small-town behavior. Maybe things were different out here.

"No, it's just that—never mind," Rae said. If he was volunteering to wash dishes, she wasn't about to say anything to stop him. "Go right ahead, wash the dishes." Then, belatedly, she added, "Thank you."

He nodded as he measured out some of the dishwashing liquid and then turned the faucet to get the water running. He watched as bubbles formed furiously, quickly filling up the sink.

"You, too," he told her.

"For what?" she asked, confused.

"Heating up dinner."

She assumed he was being sarcastic, then saw the mild expression on Sully's face and decided that maybe he wasn't.

Turning on her heel, Rae started to leave, then thought better of it. She retracted her steps and picked up a towel.

"You wash, I'll dry," she told him.

If he was surprised by her change of heart, he didn't show it.

"Sounds good to me, Mulcahy," he told her.

She studied him for a moment as she waited for him to hand her a dish to dry. "You are a really odd duck, Cavanaugh."

His mouth curved just a little. "I've been called worse."

Rae laughed shortly. "You're a police detective. I imagine you would have been." Taking the plate he held out to her, Rae dried it off quickly and placed it on the counter. She waited for him to finish the next one. "Why are you really here, Cavanaugh?"

"I already told you," he reminded her. "To clear my head." And then he looked at her as he handed her another dish. "Why? You don't believe me?"

She didn't say yes or no. Instead, she said, "You've got to admit that it's a little strange, leaving a thriving, modern city behind you to come out here and get all sweaty, wrestling with posts and digging in practically the hardest substance known to man. And I haven't even gotten around to getting you to muck out the stables."

Sully laughed. He had absolutely no doubt that she would.

"I like a challenge." She saw the handsome face become somber. "And maybe this'll help put everything else into perspective."

She could feel her curiosity being piqued. "Like what?"

Sully looked at her for a long moment. The moment stretched out so long that she thought he wasn't going to answer her.

And then, in a far quieter voice, he said, "Like there are good, decent people in the world—and more of them than there are of the other kind."

"Other kind?" Rae repeated.

She knew what he meant, but she had a feeling that something specific was eating away at him, and although she normally steered clear of personal subjects like that, his tone had a quality that made her really curious—to the point that she felt restless.

"Yeah, other kind," he confirmed, saying the words more to himself than to her.

"You mean like the people who break laws?" Rae asked him.

"You could say that." But he could see that she wanted more of an explanation than that. "People who could literally fillet the skin off another human

being and then just go on with their lives as if nothing—and I mean *nothing*—" he said the word bit-
terly "—happened."

She felt her breath backing up in her lungs.
"You're not just tossing words around, are you?"
she asked Sully quietly. One look at his face told her
that he wasn't. He was deadly serious.

"I really wish I was," he answered in an eerily
subdued voice.

Rae took a deep breath, telling herself to let him
drop the story right here, to just walk away before
this got any worse. But she found that she couldn't.
She was rooted to the spot and would remain that
way because she needed answers.

She always did.

It was her failing.

"Was this someone you were pursuing, or someone who got away?" she asked him.

He finished the last dish and handed it to her.
"Someone I was pursuing."

"And?" she asked. Rae set aside the dish he had
handed her and just looked at Sully, waiting for him
to give her more.

"And I caught him. My team and I did," he
amended, because, in the end, it had been a team
effort, although there had been a very brief period
when it had been just him and the depraved psycho-
path in that room. Along with almost an overpowering desire to wipe him off the face of the earth and
rid the world of this monster. It had taken everything

he had not to blow the man away. That's when he knew he had to get away. "Look, no disrespect, but I don't want to talk about it."

She raised her hands as if to show him that she understood what he was saying. That it was hands-off and as one human being to another, she gave him that.

"I understand," she told him in a calm voice, and for the first time since he'd met her, he felt as if they were just two people having a conversation. "Why don't you go to your room?" she told him. "I'll finish these. They're almost done, anyway."

But he shook his head and remained where he was, washing the one remaining pot as well as all the silverware that had been used at dinner. "I always finish whatever I start."

She accepted his explanation, and they worked in silence for the last few minutes until the pots and dishes were done and put away. Only then did Sully wipe off his hands and begin to leave the kitchen.

Rae stood there quietly. She was going to let him leave, but then at the last minute she called after him. "Sully."

He turned around in the doorway, raising one eyebrow. Waiting.

"Good for you," she told him.

He didn't know if she was referring to what he'd said about always finishing what he started, or if she was commenting on the fact that he had caught the killer who had terrorized so many people for a year

and a half. But he didn't ask; he just smiled and nodded before he slipped out of the room.

He'd said enough about the latter subject for now.

Chapter 7

Over the next few days, Sully found that the work on the J-H Ranch was more or less a carbon copy of the first day. His workday started at sunrise and went until sunset. After his day was over, he had dinner at the ranch house. He had breakfast there, as well. Lunch came in the form of whatever was packed into the brown bags that had been left for him and the other two men.

Daily conversation while he worked came in the form of grumbling and resentful looks from Rawlings. In Sully's estimation, the other man, Warren, wasn't much of a talker, either, but when Warren did talk, it was usually about something benign ranging from sports to how much everything seemed to cost these days. Unlike Rawlings, however, Warren didn't complain about the size—or lack thereof—of his weekly pay. He seemed satisfied with the sum.

Sully had a feeling that Warren was new to this life and that the man wasn't any more of a wrangler than he was. Still, when it came to getting the job done, Warren did the best he could and tried to hold up his end.

Rawlings made no secret of the fact that he had no use for either of them and even less for the chores that were assigned to them.

Cleaning out the stalls in the morning left him in a particularly foul mood. From what Sully could gather, Rawlings didn't much like horses. Working with them, trying to get them used to their saddles, was particularly disagreeable for him. Sully had no doubt that the horses sensed that.

"Why're you working on a horse ranch?" Sully couldn't help asking the wrangler as all three were finishing up their daily chores in the stable.

"'Cause he's afraid of cattle," Warren confided, then added in a more audible voice, "I don't much care for cattle myself. Takes next to nothing to spook a herd and start a stampede."

Not having any experience in that area, Sully had no idea if Warren was pulling his leg or sharing an actual experience.

"I'll take your word for it," he told Warren affably.

"I wouldn't take his word for anything," Rawlings declared, raising his voice from over in the far corner of an adjacent stall.

"What's he got against you?" Sully asked Warren.

The other man shrugged, his shoulders moving loosely within the shirt that appeared to be two sizes too large for him. Sully had already decided that Warren had either lost a lot of weight or was wearing someone else's castoffs. In either case, he didn't see it as really being any of his business.

"Beats me," Warren confided with a knowing smile. "Most likely the same thing he's got against everybody. He was probably one of those kids whose kindergarten teacher would've told his mama that he didn't play well with others."

The comment, completely out of left field, had Sully wondering what Warren's story was. The man definitely didn't fit in here, Sully thought. Not any more than he really did.

Although he told himself to forget about the matter, Sully couldn't help wondering about Warren and about what had prompted the man to come to Forever and to work on the ranch in the first place. He didn't seem comfortable doing any sort of ranch work. He looked happier having his head in the book that he carried around with him and opened whenever he took a break.

Although Sully had come out here to isolate himself, to just work with his hands until he'd managed to completely deplete his brain of all thought, his mind seemed to have other ideas.

It was as if he really *needed* to find some sort of a puzzle for his brain to hone it and make it sharp again.

He kept on wondering about Warren as well as

why Rawlings seemed to be both so irritated by the man and so interested in Warren at the same time.

Puzzling things out helped make the time go by for Sully.

"There's a party tomorrow at Murphy's," Rae said by way of an announcement the following Friday evening when they were all gathered at the table. "Miss Joan wanted me to tell all three of you that you're welcomed to come. The whole thing starts at five."

"Miss Joan?" Sully repeated, puzzled. "But didn't you just say that it was being held at Murphy's?"

He hadn't been off the ranch since he'd arrived, but there wasn't much to memorize when it came to Forever's locale. He knew that there was only one saloon and one place to eat, and the two didn't cross over into each other's territories. That meant that Murphy's didn't serve food and Miss Joan didn't serve alcohol in her diner. Had that suddenly changed?

"I did and it is," Rae said, finishing the last piece of fried chicken on her plate. "In keeping with her no-alcohol rule, Miss Joan decided it would be better to hold the party at Murphy's. She's having Angel make the food," Rae added quickly, anticipating the next question that one of the men might ask her—most likely Sully.

Warren looked happy about the upcoming diversion. "What's the occasion?"

"Cash and his wife are going to have another

baby—Cash is Miss Joan's stepgrandson," Rae interjected, glancing toward Sully, who she assumed might not be up on who was related to whom just yet.

"He's the town lawyer, right?" Warren asked.

"One of them," Rae answered.

For his part, Rawlings appeared less than impressed by the promise of a party or its excuse for being thrown. "Yeah, whatever."

"Well, count me in," Warren told the foreman with a happy grin. "I could definitely go for an activity that doesn't have any dirt or blisters associated with it."

"The liquor there gonna be free?" Rawlings asked, suddenly speaking up as the question occurred to him.

Rae made a calculated guess. "Probably up to a point."

Rawlings made an unintelligible sound, then said, "Yeah, well, maybe I'll come—if I'm not doing anything else."

Sully suppressed a laugh at Rawlings's qualification. From his own experience these last two weeks, there *was* nothing to do here except for work. Granted, he wasn't spending his nights in the bunkhouse—another bone of contention as far as Rawlings was concerned—but he sorely doubted that there was anything in that small building that Rawlings could find interesting enough to keep him away from a break in the combination of work and monotony.

"How about you?" Rae asked, trying not to sound

like she was interested in his answer as she looked at the newest addition to the workforce on the ranch. "Are you planning on going?"

He thought of the unexpected invitation to a party. He supposed that the people weren't really all that different, whether they were in Texas or in California. The idea of an impromptu party being thrown reminded him of his uncle Andrew back in Aurora. The former police chief had found his calling in whipping up culinary magic, and he would use any excuse imaginable to gather the family together and feed them.

Usually he didn't even need an excuse. Andrew just put the word out to come if they were in the neighborhood. And invariably it seemed like everyone almost always was.

"Sure," Sully answered. "You said five, right?"

She nodded, wiping off her fingers. "Right."

"Just who's going to be at this so-called party?" Rawlings asked suspiciously.

It seemed as if the man was *always* suspicious. About *everything*, Sully thought.

"Everyone who says yes," Rae answered simply. Then, sounding a bit annoyed, she told Rawlings, "Miss Joan didn't give me a personal accounting."

Sully wondered if the woman was any friendlier in a party setting than she appeared to be at the ranch. Finding an answer to that question was reason enough for him to attend.

"Dishwasher fixed yet?" he asked. He'd waited

until after Warren and Rawlings had left the table and gone to the bunkhouse.

Rae sighed. She'd meant to get to that, but every day there was something to make her forget until it was too late to call Mick, the town's auto mechanic and all-around repair guru.

"I haven't had time to call Mick and tell him about it." Rae pressed her lips together, relaying the information begrudgingly. She assumed that that would be the end of it.

But it wasn't.

"Mick?" Sully asked.

"He's the local mechanic," she explained, realizing that he probably didn't know that. Why should he? His car was running fine. "Mick fixes cars mostly, but he's pretty handy fixing other things as well—as long as it's nothing fancy. Why are you asking?"

"That's my roundabout way of finding out if you needed help with the dishes again." Even as he said it, he was already taking several plates into the kitchen. He placed them into the sink.

"You don't have to keep doing this," she insisted, exasperated, as she followed behind him.

"Sinking my hands into sudsy water is just about the only way I seem to be able to get the day's dirt out from under my fingernails. In a way," he said, tongue in cheek, "you're doing me a favor."

The expression on her face told him she wasn't buying that. "Well, just remember I didn't ask you to do this," she told him.

"I'll remember," Sully replied. Then, unable to suppress the question, he had to ask her. "Why do you always sound so angry about everything?"

"Why do you always ask so many questions?" Rae countered. She absolutely hated being put on the spot.

Getting the rest of the dishes and putting them into the sink, Sully shrugged in response to her question. "I guess that's just the detective in me."

Had she caught him in a lie? Rae wondered. "I thought the whole point of you being out here was for you to forget you were a detective."

"No, not forget I was a detective," Sully corrected. "Just to forget what I'd seen *as* a detective. There's a difference."

"Whatever you say," she answered, doing her best to sound totally uninterested in the subject, although in actuality, she wasn't. That was part of what was bothering her. She didn't want to take an interest in this man. Her only job was to keep this ranch running efficiently, and that meant taking care of the horses and the men only in so far as having them take care of the horses. "I don't really care."

"You didn't answer my question," he reminded her. When she merely stared at him, he repeated it. "Why do you always sound as if you're so angry about everything?"

She didn't drop her eyes from his. "Maybe because I am."

"About everything?" Sully questioned. That didn't

sound right to him unless she was a sociopath—and she wasn't.

"No, just about having people sticking their noses where they don't belong," she retorted.

"You make it hard for people to like you," he told her philosophically.

Reaching for the container of dishwashing soap underneath the sink, he measured out an amount and turned the water on. Bubbles filled the sink.

"Maybe I don't want people to like me," she told Sully.

"Everyone wants people to like them," Sully contradicted mildly.

Rae laughed harshly in response to his statement. "Tell that to Rawlings."

"Okay," Sully said agreeably, pretending to reconsider what he'd just said. "*Almost* everyone wants to be liked—at least by one person," he qualified further. And then glancing at her, he asked with a hint of a smile, "Better?"

"Better would be if you stopped talking altogether, but I guess you just can't help yourself," Rae answered as if she was resigning herself to that fact.

She grudgingly grabbed the dish Sully had just washed and was now holding out to her. The dish was wet and she'd expected that, but for some reason it seemed more slippery than the last one he had handed her, and it slipped out of her hand.

Rae made a grab for it at the same time that Sully did.

Going for it simultaneously, neither one of them

caught the dish, but they did manage to bang their foreheads against one another.

The resulting impact had them both falling backward and landing on the floor.

"I'm sorry," Sully apologized.

"No more than I am," Rae retorted, rubbing the sore spot on her forehead.

Sully tried to grab her hand to help her up, and she pulled back just as he did so. The unexpected maneuver threw him off balance. This time he would have wound up on top of Rae if, at the last minute, he hadn't anticipated that unplanned collision and managed to brace his hands on the floor on either side of her.

If anyone had looked in just then, it would look as if Sully was doing a rather erotic push-up directly over Rae's body.

Rae's heart suddenly launched into double time. "Are you planning to get up or just loom over me like that?" she asked, trying very, very hard not to sound breathless.

Sully had not only knocked the wind out of her, his close proximity had also managed to do something else. Something she hadn't been anticipating.

Something she told herself that she didn't like— but she knew she was lying to herself.

"Do you mean I have a choice?" Sully deadpanned, his face only inches from hers.

"Not if you don't want to spend the weekend walking funny," she warned him.

Sully laughed in response, something else she hadn't expected.

Before she could say another word, Sully was not only back up on his feet but helping her up to hers, as well. For just a split second, because she hadn't been prepared for it, the momentum of being helped to her feet had her body pressed up against his.

Contact had no sooner registered than Sully stepped back, putting some distance between them.

But the unexpected contact had done its damage. It had left an impression, and she felt her body tingling in response.

"Are you all right?" Sully asked. She could feel his eyes traveling over the length of her as he went on to ask, "I didn't hurt you, did I?"

"I'm fine and no, you didn't hurt me." Rae all but fired the words at him in staccato fashion, struggling to get herself under control.

What was wrong with her? she silently demanded.

"I didn't damage that happy-go-lucky disposition of yours, either, did I?" Sully asked with a touch of amusement.

Picking up the dish that was still on the floor, Rae handed it to him, a somber expression on her face. "This has to be washed again."

His eyes met hers, and he found himself struggling not to say anything. Struggling, too, not to do what he found himself wanting to do. That incredibly brief contact between them had managed to arouse things within him that he had just assumed had gone dormant.

His last manhunt had forced him to shut down nearly all of his emotions in order for him to deal with the things he had to on an almost daily basis. He couldn't allow himself to feel and do the things he had to do.

The trouble with shutting things down was that after a while, they just naturally remained that way.

And he had started to believe that they always would.

It was surprising as well as a relief to discover that he had been wrong about that.

But Sully had to admit that it was a little unnerving to have discovered all this while making unexpected bodily contact with a woman who seemed to cherish her reputation of having a tongue like a viper.

The smile on Sully's rather full lips managed to unnerve her. It was different from his usual occasional smile.

"I just handed you a dish. Why are you smiling like that?" she asked. She would have expected him to tell her to wash it herself, not to smile at her as if his soul was smiling at hers.

Sully took the dish from her and immersed it in the sink. The suds were already beginning to dissipate and fade away, leaving only discolored water to mark their passing. Looking at her over his shoulder, his smile only deepened.

Rae felt her breath standing still in her lungs and backing up in her throat.

"Why are you smiling like that?" she repeated.

He stopped washing the last dish and looked at

her, *really* looked at her, the gaze penetrating all of her defenses. Causing all sorts of things to go on within her stomach as well as the rest of her.

"You don't want to know," he answered quietly.

Chapter 8

Rae was totally taken aback by Sully's flippant statement. If there was something she hated, it was someone having preconceived notions about her and how she thought.

"Yes, I do," she insisted. "I have a right to know."

Sully slowly and deliberately wiped his hands on the dish towel that was lying crumpled on the counter. Leaving the towel there, he took a step closer to her. His eyes never left her face. "Are you sure about that?"

"I said it, didn't I?" Rae uttered the words like a challenge and tossed her head, sending her hair flying over her shoulder.

Sully inclined his head, a hint of a smile slowly making its way across his lips.

"That you did," he agreed.

It felt as if time had suddenly stopped, the moment freezing around the two people in the room. For now, the only two people in the world. Then, when time finally began to thaw out, everything that happened from then on did so in crystal-clear slow motion.

Even her heart had stopped. And then, when it began to beat again, it wasn't hammering wildly—it beat to some lyrical rhythm that she wasn't aware of ever having heard before. She was aware of it now. Very aware of it. Very aware of him.

And very aware of his lips when they finally came down on hers.

Rae didn't remember lacing her arms around his neck, didn't remember which one of them deepened the kiss. All she was aware of was that her desire had grown so deep, so overwhelming, she was in danger of drowning in it.

Shakily, Rae pulled away and tried to summon indignation, or anger, or *something* that would effectively separate her from the myriad emotions erupting all through her.

Desperately trying to collect her thoughts and get them under control, all Rae could manage to do was say, "You do realize that you just kissed your boss, don't you? Your foreman," she stressed, willing her pulse to get back into sync and stop trying to trip her up.

"I didn't kiss a foreman," Sully corrected quietly. "I kissed a very desirable woman. A woman who kissed me back."

"I did *not* kiss you back!" she protested.

She felt completely ill equipped to pull herself together. All her defenses were just out of her reach.

Sully inclined his head. "My mistake. I'm sorry,"
he told her. And then Sully left the kitchen without
another word.

Seething, Rae wanted to demand that he bring
himself right back here, that she wasn't finished talking to him. But she didn't say anything, knowing full
well what would happen if he did come back.

Sully had stirred up feelings within her, feelings
that were now clamoring for a release. And releasing them would be a very bad thing.

She had to remember not to be alone with him
like this again. At least not until she built up an im-
munity to him.

It wouldn't be easy, she told herself, but she could
do it. All it would take was vigilance. Constant vigilance.

"Did the boys bail on you?"

Rae had just arrived at Murphy's less than five
minutes ago. Miss Joan had a habit of appearing out
of nowhere within her diner.

Obviously, the woman didn't restrict herself to
doing that just at the restaurant, Rae thought.

She turned around to face the owner of the diner
and saw that Miss Joan was wearing a rather becoming two-piece navy blue dress. It was a departure
from her usual subdued way of dressing. In addition, Miss Joan had taken the time to pin her red

hair back and up, allowing a few wayward wisps to frame her face.

"I didn't see you standing there, Miss Joan. You look very pretty," Rae told her.

Miss Joan gave her a look. "Don't say it like it's a surprise, girl."

"I'm sorry, I didn't mean for it to come out sounding like that," she apologized. "Of course you always look pretty."

Miss Joan waved away the apology as well as the compliment. Instead, she focused back on what was of more interest to her. "So they're not coming?" she asked Rae.

"They said they would," Rae told the woman. "I drove separately."

Miss Joan raised one inquisitive eyebrow. "Any particular reason?"

"Yes," Rae answered. "So I can leave when I want to and not have to worry about driving a truckload of drunken wranglers back to your ranch."

Miss Joan scrutinized her for a moment, and just when Rae searched her mind, looking for a further explanation, Miss Joan said, "Very thoughtful of you, but I don't think you have to worry about that. The sheriff'll make sure that no one goes over their limit. This is a friendly celebration. He wouldn't want to see this gathering turn ugly. After all, Cash works with the sheriff's wife."

Maybe it was just her imagination, but she was prone to believing that Miss Joan had a way of being able to see right through an excuse—and she saw through hers. It wasn't that she didn't want to drive home a bunch of inebriated ranch hands—she didn't want to possibly wind up alone with Sully.

What was it her grandmother had been fond of saying? An ounce of prevention was worth more than a pound of cure. That certainly made sense in this context.

Before her interrogation could go any further, she saw Miss Joan's thin lips draw back in a knowing smile. "Well, speak of the devil."

The woman was looking directly over her shoulder toward the entrance to Murphy's. Rae turned her head even though she told herself not to.

She was just in time to see Sully walking in through the old-fashioned double swinging doors. Warren was with him, but Rawlings was nowhere to be seen.

"Wonder if he decided not to come," Rae murmured to her boss as more people came in right behind Sully and Warren.

"His loss," Miss Joan said with a dismissive shrug. "But at least Sully's here." Rae could have sworn the woman had said that for her benefit. "Well, I need to say hello to someone," she said, already moving away. Her parting words were, "Maybe you should do the same."

The words would have meant anything. But coming from Miss Joan, Rae had a feeling she knew exactly what the woman was telling her—to go greet Sully.

Even so, she avoided making eye contact with

the man. Instead, she sought out Cash and his wife, Alma. The latter had once been one of the sheriff's deputies and had the distinction of being the only woman serving in the small law enforcement department.

"Congratulations, you two," Rae said warmly, shaking Cash's hand. She was about to do the same with Alma, but the woman enfolded her in an enthusiastic embrace. Caught off guard, after a second she took a step back and looked at the other woman. "You really are glowing."

"I don't know about glowing, but I can't stop smiling," Alma told her.

"Neither can I," Cash confessed.

"Well, you both look great," Rae told the couple as she looked at them.

She was able to say only a few more words to them before someone else commandeered the couple's attention, heartily congratulating Cash and Alma on adding to their already growing family.

About to back away to let the couple mingle with their well-wishers, Rae felt a light touch on her shoulder. Even though she hadn't turned around to see who it was, every single inch of her body just knew that it was Sully.

"Hi," Sully greeted her even though they had seen one another at the ranch a little more than an hour ago. Rae had been even more distant than usual all day, and he felt that he needed to clear the air before things got any worse. "Listen, about yesterday—" he began.

Rae quickly dismissed whatever he was going to say, wanting to sweep the incident under the rug. "Already forgotten."

He surprised her by saying, "That's too bad." Stunned, she looked at him, momentarily speechless. "Because I was going to say that I found the whole experience to be very gratifying. I'm really sorry to hear that the feeling wasn't mutual. But I promise that I'll be on my best behavior," Sully added as she began to turn away.

She didn't want to come across as petulant, so she turned back to face him.

"Good," Rae responded, even though something within her felt rather disappointed and let down because he'd just said he was going to refrain from kissing her again.

You're going to drive yourself crazy, Rae, she upbraided herself.

The sound of silverware clinking against a glass suspended any further verbal exchange.

"Everyone, I'd like to propose a toast," Miss Joan's husband announced once he had gotten everyone's attention. When everyone turned toward Harry, giving the older man their undivided attention, Harry raised his glass of beer toward his grandson and granddaughter-in-law. "To the little Taylor-to-be. Aside from the day that Miss Joan made me the happiest man on earth by becoming my wife and the two days that my other great-grandchildren were born, I have to say that this ranks right up there as the happiest moment of my life." He beamed at the couple.

"May you have many more blessed events," Harry said, lifting his glass even higher.

Cash slipped his arm around Alma, drawing her closer and hugging her.

"Don't go getting ahead of yourself, Cash Taylor. We'll talk," Alma told her husband, feigning a serious expression.

Laughter rippled through the crowd.

Rae felt a deep pang. She found herself envying the couple, knowing full well that she was never going to know that kind of happiness. She had resigned herself to this life she was leading a long time ago, thinking that to want anything more would only be exceedingly ungrateful of her.

When her father had died, leaving her an orphan, she had faced a very bleak future before Miss Joan had taken her in and provided for her. To want more than she already had would just be greedy.

Liam Murphy, the youngest of the three Murphy brothers who owned and operated the bar, headlined a professional band that had just returned from a tour. Hearing about the party that was to be held at Murphy's, he'd volunteered to provide music. After Harry had given his toast and a number of other well-wishers had added a few things in its wake, Liam and his band struck up the first song.

Several couples around Rae began to dance, including Cash and Alma. Rae moved to the side, intending to get out of the couples' way. There was no official dance floor designated at Murphy's. Anywhere there was a space did just fine.

The number the band was playing had a very catchy beat, and Rae swayed to it without meaning to.

Sully observed her for a moment and then, smiling, asked, "Would you like to dance?"

Rae forced herself to stop moving to the beat. "No, that's all right."

"Don't worry, you'll be safe," he guaranteed. "In case you haven't noticed, we're out in the open." Leaning in little closer, Sully said, "And I promise not to kiss you while we're dancing."

Her chin instantly shot up defiantly. "I'm not afraid of that. Or of you."

"Oh, well that's good to hear," Sully responded. Taking one of her hands into his, he slipped his other hand around her waist. "Then let's do this," he told Rae. When she made no move to comply, he added, "Let's show them how it's done."

Despite herself, she fell into step with Sully. If she expected him to be awkward, she was disappointed. Still, she heard herself saying, "They wouldn't be dancing if they didn't know how it was done."

"You're right," he agreed with a smile. "I have so much to learn. Working for you is a complete education in itself."

Her eyebrows drew together, letting him know that she didn't find him charming, if that was what he was trying for.

She informed Sully, "I don't react well to sarcasm."

"And I've just learned something else," Sully told

her, whirling her around again before his arm tightened around her ever so slightly.

"Does that mouth of yours get you in trouble a lot where you're from?" Rae asked.

The smile on his lips widened just a little.

But it was the way he looked into her eyes that caused her stomach to tighten, hard, for a split second. She had to concentrate in order to will it to up loosen again.

"Oddly enough," he replied, "where I'm from I'm one of the quiet ones."

Yeah, right, Rae thought. "I find that very hard to believe."

Sully's smile turned into a grin. "You've got to meet my family sometime."

The song ended, but before Rae could uncouple herself from Sully, Liam and his band went right into the next number. For now, Sully gave no indication that he wanted to stop.

Resigned, Rae went on dancing with him. A second dance wouldn't hurt anything, she reasoned. Like he'd said, they were out in the open, right?

Besides, there was something in his Sully's voice when he mentioned his family that caught her attention. The mention of families always reminded her that she had none.

"Do you have a big family?" Rae asked, doing her best to sound as if she was just making conversation and that the topic wasn't close to her own heart.

Sully laughed at the question. When she looked at him quizzically, he nodded and told her, "Very big."

He'd emphasized the word *big*, further arousing her curiosity.

"How big? Five, ten people?" she guessed, thinking the latter number to be excessive.

He laughed as he shifted her so that they avoided dancing into another couple. "Not even close."

"Fifteen?" she said, growing incredulous. When he continued smiling, she guessed. "Twenty?"

He moved his head from side to side. "Keep going," he encouraged.

Okay, now he was just stringing her along. "You're exaggerating."

His grin merely grew. "Like I said, you've got to meet my family."

She was still trying to fathom the idea of having a family of ten, much less a larger one. She sighed, then grew quiet.

Sully's smile faded. Concern replaced it. "What's the matter?"

"Nothing," she tossed off. He continued looking at her, as if expecting her to explain further. She sighed again. "You're lucky, that's all. Having a big family."

Now it made sense. "There are times I would have disputed that," he told her. "But yes, now that I'm older and no longer feel as if I'm hopelessly outnumbered, I agree with you. I *am* lucky. You don't get along with your family?"

A few days ago, she would have told him to mind his own business, but being here at the party, dancing with him like this, changed a few things, so she answered him. "I don't have a family to get along with."

"You don't have a family?" he asked. He couldn't begin to understand what that had to be like. While sympathetic, he had no frame of reference to fall back on. There had *always* been family around for him. "What about Miss Joan?" The woman wasn't exactly sugar and vanilla spice, but she did seem to have a soft spot when it came to Rae.

This time Rae did smile. "She's more like my fairy godmother, and I care about her a lot, but she's not a relative."

"Fairy godmother, huh?" He glanced over toward the woman who now appeared to be ordering Brett Murphy around. "There's a bedtime story in the making," he said with a dry laugh.

She took offense for the woman who had been like a second mother to her.

"Don't you dare say anything bad about Miss Joan," she warned him. "That woman took me in when she didn't have to."

"I wouldn't dream of it," he told her. "Besides, Uncle Seamus would have my head if I said one negative word against that woman." He grinned again. "I've grown very attached to my head."

Rae groaned at the pun and smiled despite herself.

"Knew you had it in you," Sully told her.

"Knew I had *what* in me?"

"A smile," Sully said, suddenly whirling her around on the floor. Rae didn't pull back or stop dancing.

As far as Sully was concerned, the tempo for the evening had been set.

Chapter 9

Rae had had every intention of only staying at the party for a little while, a couple of hours at best. But the party turned out to be better than she'd expected, and having Sully at her side seemed to somehow enhance that good time.

Sully managed to get her to remain at the party until it was officially over.

And it wasn't that Sully monopolized her. While never seeming to leave her side, Sully still mingled with everyone else who had attended—and those people mingled with Rae, as well.

Rae interacted with more people in the space of those few hours than she had over the course of more than the last year.

It was one whirlwind of an evening as far as Rae

was concerned. And it had showed her a side of Sully Cavanaugh that she hadn't known existed. He was downright friendly and charming.

As they got ready to leave in their separate vehicles, Rae felt she had to make an observation.

"You know, for a man who came out here with the intention of keeping to himself, you certainly did an about-face rather fast."

Sully looked around. A good many of the guests had already left—and, he realized, he had talked to most of them.

"I guess I sort of did," he agreed. "All these people gathering together to celebrate Miss Joan's grandson and daughter-in-law's coming baby just reminded me of my own family. There was always some celebration or other being thrown." He smiled fondly as he recalled the last few. "I got so caught up in all the bad things I saw going on recently, I forgot to focus on all the good there was right there in front of me."

Rae saw the expression in his eyes as he mentioned his family and drew her own conclusion. "So that means you'll be leaving soon?"

She had no idea why that would hit her so hard. After all, she was used to wranglers coming and going on the ranch on a regular basis. It was practically a way of life, and it just reinforced her feelings that she couldn't really count on anyone but herself. Why Sully leaving should bother her so much made no sense to her.

And yet there was a knot in her stomach.

"Oh no," he said as they walked out together and

went behind Murphy's. When he'd pulled his truck in earlier, the lot had been fairly crowded. Now it was all but cleared out, he noted. "I signed on to work on the ranch for at least a month. Longer if the job's not finished. I have no intentions of leaving before then."

She felt the knot loosening, at least for now.

Can't get used to this, she warned herself. *He's gonna be leaving soon enough. The man has a life back in California.*

"That's good. I mean, I won't have to tell Miss Joan she needs to be on the lookout for someone else to send in. But I think you should realize that around here, the work is *never* finished. If you're lucky, you don't find yourself overwhelmed." She allowed herself a small, tight smile. "You've done more work than those two drifters have done in all the time they've been here. Though he does try, Warren's kind of inept, and as for Rawlings, well, there's no good way to put this." She'd given him more than a dozen chances, and the man still wound up disappointing her each and every time. "He's just plain lazy."

Sully made no comment about Rawlings, but the mention of Warren had him looking around the parking lot.

"Speaking of Warren, have you seen him?" Sully asked. "I didn't see him among the few people who were left inside. I felt positive that he'd be waiting out here by my truck."

"You're his ride?" she asked, trying to remember if she had seen the two entering together. All she could recall was seeing Sully and no one else.

"Yeah, I brought him to the dance," Sully confirmed with a grin.

"Maybe he caught a ride back with someone else," Rae suggested. She thought for a moment. "Come to think about it, I don't remember seeing him around in the last couple of hours. Maybe he decided not to stay and left early."

"You're probably right, but I'm going to go inside and check again just in case," he told her. "I'd hate to leave him stranded after I brought him out here." Starting to leave, Sully stopped long enough to tell her, "You don't have to wait here until I get back. You should get going. Just be careful driving home."

"Just like I've been doing for the last thirteen years," she pointed out.

Ordinarily, if someone said that to her, she would have felt insulted that the person thought of her as too inept to make it back to the ranch. But the odd thing was that she didn't feel insulted. Instead, she found it rather sweet that Sully was concerned about her welfare.

She wasn't sure what to make of it.

The man was definitely confusing her, she thought as she watched him walk back inside Murphy's.

Instead of leaving, she stayed where she was. Rae decided to linger to see if he had any luck locating Warren. After all, Warren did work for her.

"Brett said he saw Warren leaving more than two hours ago," Sully told her when he came out of Murphy's a few minutes later.

He thought it rather strange that the man hadn't said anything to him when he was leaving, seeing as how he'd been Warren's ride.

"Problem solved," Rae declared. Taking one look at the pensive expression on Sully's face, she surmised, "Problem not solved?"

Sully shrugged. He was probably making too much of this, seeing problems when none really existed. Still, something was bothering him about this. "It's just kind of strange, that's all."

"I won't argue with that. Now you can be my escort home," she told him, getting into her truck. "So to speak. I'll see you at the ranch house."

She took off before Sully could answer her.

Reminding himself that he wasn't the other wrangler's keeper, he couldn't shake the feeling that something was off.

That would be the famous Cavanaugh gut, he silently thought, laughing at himself. There was no law that said everything had to make sense.

He just preferred it that way.

Sully kept an eye out for any sign of another vehicle on the road despite the fact that the saloon owner had told him that Warren had left Murphy's over two hours ago. If he saw another vehicle on the side of the road now, that would have meant that Warren and whoever was giving him a ride back had broken down.

But there was no sign of another vehicle anywhere around on the way back to the ranch, and no sign of Warren, either.

* * *

The house was quiet when Sully finally walked in. He took that to mean that Rae had turned in for the night. He would have liked to talk to her for a while longer just to wind down, but on second thought, maybe it was better this way. If Rae was still up, they'd be alone together, and he just might be tempted to see if perhaps they could pick up where they had left off the other night.

And that might really complicate things, he thought.

Definitely better this way, he silently insisted, perhaps a little more emphatically than was necessary.

It was late and he needed to turn in. He had a feeling that tomorrow was going to be a very long day. There really was no such thing, he'd come to learn, as a day off on a horse ranch. If you weren't there for part of the day, you just got to work that much harder the next.

Sully wasn't sure how long he'd been at work when Rae walked into the stables. About to say hello to her, she cut him short by asking, "Have you seen Warren?"

"No, but then I didn't swing by the bunkhouse," Sully reminded her. "I came straight to the stables this morning to get a head start on the work. Why?" He noticed the odd expression on her face. "Something wrong?"

Rae frowned. "When you didn't come to breakfast, I thought you were gone, too."

"I just grabbed a couple of slices of toast to go. I had a feeling that Rawlings hadn't held up his end and that there'd be a lot to do today." Sully stopped abruptly as her words replayed themselves in his head. "What do you mean 'gone, too'?" And then he made a guess as to whom she was talking about. "Rawlings's gone?"

"No." Her tone sounded that she wished he was. "I left him in the kitchen, gorging himself on waffles. He told me that Warren never came in last night."

"Never came in?" Sully echoed as he stopped working. "But he left Murphy's around seven— maybe eight. He left way before we did."

"Well, he didn't seem to make it home." Rae shrugged, looking impatient. "There's probably nothing to worry about. I mean, he's taken off before. Except that maybe this time he just kept going." She sighed, shaking her head. "If I had to lose someone, I would rather it had been Rawlings. At least Warren tried to do the work, even though the man was totally out of his element."

She was marching around now, like a tiger seeking release, Sully thought. "What *was* his element?"

She shook her head. "I have no idea. He never talked about where he came from or what he did for a living before he turned up here. But Miss Joan seemed to think that he needed a second chance and I wasn't about to question that. I mean, after all, she took me in. Although I think she missed the boat with Rawlings." She thought that over. "I suppose in his defense, he only started to slack off after Warren came here."

Sully looked at her curiously. "They didn't arrive here together?" He had just assumed that they did.

"No. Rawlings was here a whole month before Warren turned up," she told him.

Since there was no sign of Rawlings coming to join him in the stables, Sully got back to work. The stalls weren't going to clean themselves.

"Did you check his bunk?" he asked Rae. When she didn't answer, he clarified, "To see if he took his things."

They'd been through this once before, and she was annoyed with herself for not remembering to do that. She threw "No, I didn't," over her shoulder as she left the stables.

Sully was still working—and still doing it on his own—when Rae returned fifteen minutes later. One look at her face had him abandoning the last stall and crossing over to her.

"What's the matter?" he asked. "Did you kill him?" He was referring to Rawlings, trying to get a smile out of her. He didn't succeed. Her scowl deepened.

"No, and Warren's things are gone," she said. "He packed up and left. This is *not* a good time to take off like this. The least he could have done was tell me. It doesn't make any sense," she complained. "The man didn't seem unhappy, just out of his element."

"But he was grateful for the work," she added.

"If Rawlings had taken off like this, I wouldn't have been surprised. But Warren…" Her voice trailed off, underscoring her confusion.

"Did you question Rawlings?" Sully asked. "Did he happen to see who gave Warren the ride back to the ranch?"

"What's the point?" she retorted. "It doesn't matter who gave him a ride from Murphy's. It wasn't to the ranch. Rawlings said he didn't see Warren. He's gone now."

Didn't she understand? "That's exactly *why* it does matter. Maybe he intended to come back but whoever gave him that ride had other ideas."

"We don't know *what* happened," she pointed out. "Maybe Warren did come back. He came back, packed up and took off in that old jeep he drove when he first came into Forever."

Sully pieced together the spare information that they did have. "But Rawlings never came to Murphy's yesterday. That means he was here the entire time. He told you that he didn't see Warren, which means Warren never came back to the ranch."

"But he had to have come back," she realized. "I just said that his things were missing."

"So either Rawlings lied about not seeing him or Warren came back when Rawlings wasn't around and took his things," Sully concluded. "Where did you say Rawlings was now?"

This needed further investigating, he thought, leaning the shovel he'd been using to clean out the stalls against one of the walls.

"He's probably still in the kitchen, eating breakfast like he hadn't had anything to eat for the last three days," she told him, frowning.

Sully started to walk to the ranch house. Rae was right behind him, walking quickly in order to keep up with his longer stride.

"Do you remember what time it was when you last saw Warren?" Sully asked Rawlings.

"How should I know?" Rawlings demanded. "I don't mark these things down."

But Sully was not about to just back off. "Was it when he left with me for Miss Joan's party at Murphy's?" he asked more forcefully.

Looking a little unnerved by Sully's tone, Rawlings shrugged as he shifted his chair back. "That sounds right, I guess."

"Why didn't you come to Murphy's?" Sully asked. "The invitation was for everyone. Man like you would find free beer and free food pretty tempting."

"I decided not to go, okay?" the wrangler answered defensively. "I thought after working all week I just wanted to kick back and relax. With Warren gone to this thing, I didn't have to put up with mindless conversation."

Sully seemed to draw in closer, all but in Rawlings's face. "And you didn't see him after that?"

"I already told you said I didn't," Rawlings retorted angrily. He turned to face the foreman. "Look, I don't exactly get paid much. Do I have to put up with him firing questions at me like I'm guilty of something before he even tells me what the hell's going on?"

"We think Warren's missing," Rae told the other man, begrudgingly doling out her words.

Rawlings looked unimpressed. "Maybe he just took off again, like last time."

"He took his things with him, cleared out his locker," Sully told the wrangler.

"Then maybe he took off for good. Can't say I blame him," Rawlings said. "If I had somewhere to go, maybe I'd take off for good, too."

"A man just doesn't take off without saying something. You said you have a decent relationship with him," Sully said, looking at Rae.

"I do—or did," she corrected. "Warren was really trying to do better."

"Then something must have spooked him," Sully speculated. "Was there anyone at the party you didn't recognize?" he asked her. "Like a stranger? Someone who Warren might have known from his past? It was pretty crowded there at the high point."

Rae shook her head. "No, I didn't see anyone like that at Murphy's. Everyone there was from Forever."

"You're not," Rawlings pointed out, glaring at Sully.

Rae was quick to turn the accusation back at the wrangler. "Neither are you."

"Yeah, but I wasn't there," Rawlings reminded them. "I was right here, on the ranch, minding my own business, remember?"

For now, Sully ignored the irritating cowboy.

"Maybe Warren'll change his mind and come back. Maybe this is all just a big misunderstanding and he's spending time with someone after the party. I'm going to go back to work—" he began.

"I could file a missing-persons report on Warren with the sheriff," she said, thinking out loud.

"You can't," he told her matter-of-factly. "You have to wait at least twenty-four hours before filing a missing-persons report. By my count it's only been about half that time."

She looked at him impatiently. "That might be true in California and even in some of the bigger cities in Texas. But Forever's got different rules," she informed him. "Out here someone's missing when they *go* missing."

He could see there was no arguing with her about this. He also saw that despite the front she put up, Rae was worried that something had happened to Warren.

"All right then, why don't you go and file that report with the sheriff," he told her. Stripping off the gloves he'd been using, he stuck them in his back pocket. "I'll go with you."

"You don't have to," she retorted.

His eyes met hers. "I have to" was all he said.

Nodding, she turned toward the other wrangler. "All right. Rawlings, you get to spend another day by yourself—with the horses," she added.

The wrangler looked less than thrilled. "You're leaving me here to do all the work?"

"You catch on quick," Rae said as she left with Sully.

In the background, Rawlings muttered something unintelligible under his breath. Because she was worried about Warren, she let it go.

Chapter 10

Sheriff Rick Santiago looked up from the report he was reading on his desk. He looked mildly surprised to see who had just walked into his inner office.

"Morning, Rae," the sheriff said, half rising from his chair. His eyes shifted to the man who had walked in right behind her. "Sully, right?" he asked.

Sully had a feel that Forever's sheriff was far sharper than the laid-back, easygoing image he liked projecting.

Putting his hand out to the dark-haired man, Sully shook hands with him. "Right. We met last night."

Rick's smile was benign as it took in both visitors. "So, what can I do for you, Rae?"

Rae took a breath, as if she needed to fortify herself before speaking. "This is an official visit."

Rick gestured toward the two chairs in front of his desk. "Have a seat," he told them, doing the same. Once his visitors had gotten comfortable, he said, "Okay, tell me what official thing brings you here?"

Rae sat up a little straighter. "One of the latest wranglers Miss Joan had me take on at the ranch has gone missing."

Interest flickered across the sheriff's suntanned face. This was different than the usual things that his office was asked to handle. For the most part, those involved missing livestock and occasional acts of vandalism brought on by one of the citizens having had too much to drink and then getting pulled into a meaningless argument with another Forever resident.

"Who is it?"

"John Warren," Rae answered.

Pulling a pad closer, he made a note on it. "How long has Warren been missing?" Rick asked.

"Since sometime yesterday afternoon," she answered. She saw minor surprise cross the sheriff's face. "He came to Miss Joan's party at Murphy's along with everyone else, but then I lost track of him."

Rick raised his brow, looking from Rae to her companion. "Were you supposed to be keeping track of him?" he asked, obviously thinking this was rather an odd choice of words.

This wasn't the point, Rae thought, annoyed that the sheriff wasn't focusing on what was important. "No, but, well, some of the people who Miss Joan

Dear Reader,

IT'S A FACT: if you answer 4 quick questions, we'll send you **4 FREE REWARDS!**

I'm not kidding you. As a leading publisher of women's fiction, we value your opinions... and your time. That's why we are prepared to **reward** you handsomely for completing our mini-survey. In fact, we have 4 Free Rewards for you, including 2 free books and 2 free gifts.

As you may have guessed, that's why our mini-survey is called **"4 for 4".** Answer 4 questions and get 4 Free Rewards. It's that simple!

Thank you for participating in our survey,

Pam Powers

To get your 4 FREE REWARDS:
Complete the survey below and return the insert today to receive 2 FREE BOOKS and 2 FREE GIFTS guaranteed!

"4 for 4" MINI-SURVEY

1 Is reading one of your favorite hobbies?

☐ YES ☐ NO

2 Do you prefer to read instead of watch TV?

☐ YES ☐ NO

3 Do you read newspapers and magazines?

☐ YES ☐ NO

4 Do you enjoy trying new book series with FREE BOOKS?

☐ YES ☐ NO

YES! I have completed the above Mini-Survey. Please send me my 4 FREE REWARDS (worth over $20 retail). I understand that I am under no obligation to buy anything, as explained on the back of this card.

240/340 HDL GNUV

FIRST NAME   LAST NAME

ADDRESS

APT.#   CITY

STATE/PROV.   ZIP/POSTAL CODE

decides need a second chance aren't always exactly Boy Scout material—"

"In my experience, I don't think that any of them are—" his eyes shifted to Sully "—present company excepted." Pausing, he wanted to get something clear up in his mind. "You're a police detective, aren't you?"

Instead of answering directly, Sully had his own question for the sheriff. "Miss Joan tell you that?"

"This is a small town, Detective," Rick told him. "Gossip is one of these people's main source of entertainment."

Taking the answer in stride, Sully asked the sheriff, "And just what does local gossip have to say about Warren?"

"Not much, actually," Rick admitted. "Some speculation of course, but nothing concrete." And then he added, "Not like with Rawlings."

"What about Rawlings?" The question came from Rae, who had slid to the edge of her seat, eager for any sort of an answer.

"Well, the man's not exactly a candidate for sainthood," Rick told her.

"Was he ever convicted of any felonies?" Sully asked.

"From what I gathered, Rawlings's guilty of finding ways of bilking people out of their hard-earned money, but so far, there's nothing on record that anyone could make stick. And he's been clean since he got here," the sheriff added. He saw the somewhat dubious look on Sully's face. "This might be a small town, but we're not simpletons. Some of us even know how to operate those newfangled boxy-looking things called a computer, or some such thing."

"That wasn't surprise you saw on my face, Sheriff," Sully told him. "That was just admiration."

Rick laughed. "I'm just having a little fun with you, Sully. Like I said, we don't have much by way of diversion around here."

"About my missing ranch hand," Rae said, trying to get the sheriff back on track.

"Sorry," Rick apologized, looking at her earnestly. "Do you have any reason to suspect that your wrangler might have met with some foul play?"

Rae looked at the sheriff, taken aback by the question. "I haven't even thought of that."

"Then why are you here?" Rick asked. He didn't seem to understand what would have prompted her to report the man missing so quickly if she didn't think something bad had happened to him. "Did he take something from the ranch before he disappeared?"

She flushed slightly, knowing her negative answer didn't carry any weight. "Nothing's missing that I can see. I didn't take a full inventory, but then, there's nothing much to inventory."

"How do you know he's gone?" Rick asked. "Maybe Warren just got lucky at the party and decided to spend the night with a new friend." He looked at her, curious to see how this scenario went over with Rae. "Things like that have been known to happen."

"His things are gone," Sully told the sheriff, answering for Rae. "His clothes and whatever he kept in that knapsack he had under his bunk."

Rae turned to look at him. "You knew about the knapsack?" she asked, surprised. "I thought you didn't go into the bunkhouse."

"I never said that," he pointed out. Sully was aware that both sets of eyes were now looking at him. "I always like to take in my surroundings when I'm in a new place," he explained.

Armed with this new information, Rick turned toward Sully. "Any idea what Warren had in that knapsack?" he asked.

But Sully had to shake his head. "I didn't look inside."

More than mild surprise registered on the sheriff's face. "You weren't *curious*?"

"Sure," Sully admitted, "but a man's entitled to his privacy. I figured the knapsack probably just contained an extra change of clothes, maybe some memento to remind him of where he came from."

Rick nodded. "Most likely," he agreed. Sighing, he reviewed what had just been said. "Well, unless you're willing to fill out a statement saying that Warren robbed you or there's any evidence of foul play, there's really nothing I can do. A person can just take off if they find the situation doesn't suit them for one reason or another. There's no law against that." He flashed Rae a contrite smile. "Sorry."

Rae suppressed a sigh. "That's all right," she said. She got up out of her chair. "I'm probably just overreacting."

Taking his cue from her, Sully rose to his feet, as well.

"Let me know if Warren suddenly comes wandering back," Rick told her.

"Will do," Rae promised as she left the office. Crossing the floor to reach the outer door, she nodded at the deputies she passed. There were two of them in the office. The senior deputy, Joe Lone Wolf, was out patrolling the town.

"Problem?" Deputy Gabe Rodriguez asked her as she walked by.

"Apparently not," Rae answered. She just kept on walking until she was out of the sheriff's office.

"You don't feel better, do you?" Sully guessed once they were outside.

She knew that saying no wasn't enough in this case. "I guess what I'm feeling is betrayed," she admitted. "Not by the sheriff," she was quick to add to prevent a misunderstanding. "By Warren. I was nice to that man—I looked the other way when he made mistakes and waited until he found his way. And then he just takes off, just like that!"

"Being nice to someone should be its own reward," Sully told her. "Think about it. You weren't nice to Warren because you expected something in return. You were nice to him because you felt he'd been knocked around by life and maybe if he was treated like a human being, he'd realize that everyone isn't just out for themselves. That there are decent people around."

She spared him a frown as they went back to her

truck. "They teach philosophy at that police department of yours?" she asked as she got back behind
the wheel.

"No," he answered, getting into the truck's cab
on the passenger side. "That's the sort of thing you
develop when you're a Cavanaugh."

She started up the truck but left it in Park for a
moment as she looked at him. "I don't know whether
to feel sorry for you or envy you."

"Whatever makes you feel comfortable," Sully
advised her.

Rae was surprised at his answer. After a beat, she
told him, "I'll give it some thought."

Almost a week went by, and there was still no
sign of Warren returning.

"I guess he decided that ranch work wasn't for
him," Sully speculated, raising his voice so that
Rawlings could hear him above the wind and the
rain.

The latter looked angry about having to work hard
and bit off a retort.

The shift in the weather had been totally unexpected, darkening the skies several hours before
nightfall.

When the rain hit hard, the horses were all still
out in the corral. Sully and Rawlings hurried to try
to bring the animals in out of the rain as quickly as
possible. Several of the horses in the corral were
yearlings and hadn't been tamed yet. They were particularly skittish in this storm. When Sully tried to

bring them into the stable, one of the horses bolted and took off.

Seeing the other ranch hand just stand there, letting loose with a string of colorful curses, Sully had no choice but to take after the fleeing horse before it was either lost or wound up getting badly hurt through some mishap.

The truck was back near the ranch house. Thinking quickly, Sully picked up the rope that was looped over on the corral's gate and secured it over his shoulder. He grabbed closest horse by the mane, swung onto the stallion bareback and took off after the yearling that already had a head start on him.

Riding hard and grateful for those summers Seamus had indulged his fantasy and taken him riding, Sully finally managed to corner the frightened yearling near a grove of trees.

Sliding off his horse, Sully approached the other animal slowly, talking to it in a calm, low cadence. As he talked, his eyes never leaving the yearling, he removed the rope he'd slung over his shoulder and formed a lasso. He intended to slip it over the yearling's head and use it to eventually lead the frightened animal back to the stable behind his own horse.

"It's okay, boy. I know you're scared. There's all this noise all over the place and this wet stuff coming down, making you sopping wet. But I promise none of that will hurt you. *I* won't hurt you," he said, inching closer. "You need to come back with me to that nice, warm, dry stall of yours. There's this big bag of feed waiting just for you. Doesn't that sound nice, boy? All you can eat?

"Now all you've got to do is let me put this little lasso around your neck so that I can lead you back to your stall. Nothing hard about that, right, boy?"

But when he finally reached the runaway, the frightened yearling reared on his hind legs, his front hooves pawing the air and then coming down hard on the ground.

The ground where they were was even more unlevel than in most spots. The yearling almost tripped and fell. He looked really frightened again. Whinnying, he almost fell a second time.

Righting himself again, the yearling took off, heading away from the ranch house and the stable.

Sully was just about to get back up on his mount and take off after the runaway for a second time when he inadvertently look down on the ground.

Blinking, he looked down again, convinced that he had to be imagining things. Between the inclement weather and the progressively darkening sky, he felt that his eyes were playing tricks on him and it was easy to see what wasn't there.

Except that this time it was.

Sully leaned in for a closer look and was about to get down on the ground when he heard the sound of approaching hoofbeats. Whirling around, he didn't know what to expect. On his guard, he automatically reached for his weapon—a weapon he hadn't had on him since he'd come out to Forever.

Feeling only the unsatisfactory touch of material, he cursed. "Damn it!"

"Is that meant for me?" Rae asked, reaching him and dismounting.

Sully exhaled then took in a deep breath, bracing himself. He hadn't wanted her to see this until he had a chance to talk to her.

"I didn't know you were out here," he told Rae, which was true.

"Clearly," Rae answered. "Which way did the yearling go?" she asked, ready to swing back into her saddle and give chase.

He knew she wouldn't forgive him if he didn't tell her about his discovery now that she was right here, standing practically on top of it.

Starting slowly, he felt his way around the subject. "Before you take after the yearling, I think you should know that my horse came really close to falling and possibly breaking his leg."

Rae looked at him skeptically. "Now who's exaggerating?"

"Not me."

Sully said the words with such conviction, Rae held off riding after the runaway horse. She could see that he was circling around a subject, trying to tell her something.

"Is that supposed to make me feel better?" When he said nothing, she had to ask, "What's going on, Sully?"

Moving his mount aside, Sully crouched down near the area where the horse had almost slipped.

The rain was falling even harder now, turning the ground into mud. Digging in it promised to be even messier now than it originally had.

Even so, he began to dig with his hands.

The soil had recently been disturbed and, from what he could see, replaced. It wasn't nearly as hard as the ground where he had replaced those posts for the fence had been.

Rae stared at him. "What are you doing?" she asked. Her horse was getting antsy, moving from side to side. It was obvious that her mare wanted to gallop off.

"I'm digging," Sully answered, raising his voice.

"I can see that," she answered. He really did try her patience, she thought. Nothing was every straightforward with Sully. "Why? What are you looking for?"

"I don't know," he answered honestly. "But this soil was recently disturbed, and there doesn't seem to be a reason for that."

She reminded herself that he was, after all, a city kid and as such, unfamiliar with the creatures that made their home out here.

"Look, this place is full of all sorts of wild animals," she told him. "Animals dig. Some of them bury their kill to keep other animals from eating whatever they brought down until they can get back to it. That's probably all this is," she said, waving her hand at the area he was digging up. "You're wasting your time, Cavanaugh."

Sully assumed she was lamenting the time he was losing by doing this.

"I'll work to make it up," he promised as he went on digging. "You can probably catch up to that yearling. It looked spooked enough to run around in circles."

She knew he was probably right and that she should go after the runaway. But something kept her right where she was.

Rethinking her position, Rae got down on her knees beside Sully, sinking her hands into the wet soil as she dug alongside him.

Looking at the soaking-wet soil, she asked, "This was fresh, wasn't it?"

The ground had been disturbed, but so far, he hadn't found anything, and he was starting to wonder if maybe he was wrong in thinking what he'd been thinking. "It certainly looked that way."

"This looks like it's a large mound. Too big for an animal to have buried whatever's here on its own," she commented, keeping her head down and trying to keep the rain from getting into her eyes.

Sully shook his head, agreeing with her. "I don't think an animal buried this. At least, not your usual kind of animal."

And that was when he uncovered it. Brushing the mud back with his grimy hands, Sully unearthed what he hadn't bargained for.

John Warren.

Chapter 11

Sully heard the really sharp intake of breath behind him. Turning to look at Rae, he saw absolutely stunned horror on her face. He expected the woman to scream once what she was looking at registered.

But Rae just bit down on her lip. Bit down so hard that for a second, he felt sure that she was going to draw blood.

Grabbing her by her shoulders, Sully pulled her up to her feet. He held Rae pressed against him in an effort to block her line of vision.

"Don't look," he ordered.

But instead of hiding her face in his shoulder, she turned her head, looking at the lifeless body more than half submerged in mud.

"Too late," she whispered. Sully could feel her

shaking against him. Even so, Rae put her hands up against his chest, intent on pushing him back. "I'm a big girl," she insisted almost defensively.

"That doesn't mean you need to look at something grotesque and horrible," Sully argued, still attempting to shield her from having to look at the dead man.

Rae took in a shaky breath, attempting to get herself under control. "I've already seen him. I can't pretend to unsee him."

Reluctantly, Sully released his hold on her shoulders. But he remained close enough to grab her in case Rae experienced a delayed reaction and passed out.

"Well, at least we know why he didn't come back." Sully could tell she was still struggling not to allow shock to overwhelm her. Even in the rain, her face looked exceptionally ashen. Rae swallowed to keep her voice calm. "What do you think happened?"

"I didn't see his truck around here." Sully took a calculated guess. "Maybe he was out here for some reason and got lost."

"Why would he even be out here in the first place?" Rae shook her head. "That doesn't make any sense."

He agreed, but now wasn't the time to examine theories.

"We can try to figure this out later," he told her. Glancing back at the part of the wrangler that was exposed, he said, "Right now, I'm going to dig all of him up and get the sheriff to take over." Since he didn't have a shovel or anything else to use, Sully began to dig in the mud with his hands. "Technically, this is his jurisdiction."

She wasn't so ready to just hand the investigation off and keep out of the way. "Warren was working on the ranch, and that makes it my jurisdiction."

Rae said it with such feeling, he stopped digging for a second.

"What are you saying?"

"I owe it to Warren to find out what happened to him—and why," she added.

He studied her expression for a moment. She was serious. "It could have just been a simple matter of getting lost."

Rae frowned. "You don't believe that, either, do you?"

By using the word *either* he assumed that she was including herself. But he wasn't about to fan any flames just yet. She needed to calm down a little first.

"I work with facts," he told her. "The fact is that we know the man is dead, but we don't know anything else about this."

"Yet," she emphasized.

He knew that meant she intended to find out. He wasn't about to let her do that alone.

"Yet," Sully agreed. "Look, why don't you see if you can reach the sheriff and get him out here while I go on digging Warren out? The storm might interfere with your reception, but it's worth a shot trying to get through."

Rae nodded and moved to the side. Sully contin-

ued digging as fast as he could even though the mud
and the rain weren't making it easy for him.

When he had exposed the upper third of the dead
man's body, Sully sank his hands deeper into the
mud until he was able to encircle his arms around
Warren. Bracing himself, he yanked the rest of the
man's body out of the mud. Dragging Warren's body
over several more feet, he didn't stop until he managed to get it under the partial cover of a large tree.

Spent, Sully collapsed onto the soggy ground. His
heart was pounding, and he concentrated on catching
his breath. After a minute, he became more aware of
his surroundings. He saw Rae closing her phone and
slipping it back into the pocket of her jacket.

She made her way over to him. He noticed her deliberately looking at the muddied body, as if daring
herself not to look away. It was as if she wouldn't
allow herself to be soft. She wasn't an easy person
to read, he thought.

"Sheriff's on his way," she told him. Then she finally looked at him instead of the dead man. "You
all right?"

"Better than he is," Sully answered, nodding at
the dead man. "By the way," he asked as an afterthought hit him, "where's Rawlings?"

She had to think. It seemed like it had all happened a hundred years ago.

"I left him in the stable and told him to feed the
horses." She laughed drily. "He's probably still there.
That man can draw out any chore to make it last all
day." She looked over toward Warren's body again.

Seeing him like that didn't get any easier, she thought grimly. "Rawlings wouldn't have been any help digging Warren up," she said, thinking that was why Sully had asked about the wrangler's whereabouts.

"Oh, I'm sure of that," Sully agreed. "I just thought he could have gone after that runaway."

With all of this going on, she had completely forgotten about the yearling.

Rae flushed. "Oh Lord, he's still out there." Getting up, she made a futile attempt to brush the mud off her legs, then gave up. "I'd better go try to find him before he gets lost."

Sully was on his feet instantly and got in front of her to keep her from leaving.

"I don't think that's a very good idea," he told her. "It's getting darker, and I don't think you should be out there by yourself right now. Not until we find out exactly what happened to Warren."

She didn't like being told what to do, but for now she ignored that reaction and focused on something else. "Then you *do* think it's foul play?"

He wasn't about to let himself be pinned down just yet. "Like I said, right now we don't know what to think, but the man didn't just bury himself, which means that foul play is a very real possibility." He looked at her sternly. "Which in turn means being cautious."

Running the ranch had her always putting her own needs last and focusing on what needed to be done. "What about the yearling? There are wolves out there, and he could become some wolf's dinner."

Sully could see that if he didn't do something about the missing horse, she was going to take off looking for it.

"I tell you what. As soon as the sheriff gets here, I'll fill him in and then go look for the runaway." He looked to see if that worked for her. "Okay?"

"If you insist on going to look for the yearling, why don't you go now?" she asked. "I can tell the sheriff how you found the body, and I'm not afraid to sit watch over a dead man." To her that was a simple solution.

But Sully had no intention of budging. "I don't want to leave you alone out here, either."

She thought she heard something ominous in Sully's voice. "Do you know more than you're telling me, Cavanaugh?"

"No."

Her eyebrows drew together as she tried to fathom his thinking. "Then why—"

Anticipating her question, Sully cut her off before she could say anything further. "It's my background. It makes me cautious, all right?"

His answer didn't go down well with her. "I don't need you being cautious for me, Cavanaugh."

He pulled his lips back in a smile she found patronizing. "Consider it a bonus for letting me work here."

Her dark look continued. "That wasn't up to me," she told him. "That was all Miss Joan's doing."

The last of his patience evaporated. "Damn it, woman, does everything have to be an argument with you?" he asked, struggling to get his temper under control again. It wasn't working. "You would *really* fit in with my family, especially my sisters. All of you could readily argue the ears off a brass monkey."

Sully was about to say something else when he looked at her more closely. Leaning in, he saw that there were tears in her eyes.

"You're crying," Sully realized, instantly regretting his tone. "Hey, I didn't mean to—"

Unable to speak for a second without having her voice break, she gestured for Sully to stop talking. Rae waved her hand before his face until she could finally get herself under control.

"No, it's not you," she managed to get out. "I was just…just thinking about Warren. I never got to know…to know *anything* about him and now he's dead." She paused for a second to get herself further under control, then went on. "I don't even know if he has any family, or who to notify that he's…that he's…"

She couldn't bring herself to finish.

Sully started to take her into his arms, just one human being attempting to comfort another. But she fought him, putting her hands up again, this time against his chest, to hold him at bay.

"I don't need you to comfort me," Rae protested, an angry hitch in her voice.

"Maybe I need you to comfort me," Sully told her quietly. Then his arms closed around her.

She made a noise, and it sounded like she was

going to tell him off. But she didn't. This time, she didn't even try to push him away or to block his arms from closing around her.

Resting her head against his shoulder, she struggled to keep her sobs back. "This isn't…a sign…of…weakness."

"No one said it was," he replied quietly.

Sully stood there holding her until she stopped crying.

Once she did, Rae drew back and then drew in a shaky, stabilizing breath.

"This is just between us," she warned him.

He cocked his head, as if considering her words. "I guess I'll just have to skip my byline in your weekly newspaper," he replied.

A laugh almost escaped her lips in response. "Anybody ever tell you you're a smart-ass?" she asked, secretly very grateful that he wasn't going to say anything about her temporary break to anyone.

"Only on days that end in a *y*," he told her.

"Well, then allow me add my voice to that."

The rain was finally beginning to let up when they heard a horse whinny. At first Sully thought the sound was coming from his stallion, but then he saw that there was a shadow just beyond the perimeter of the area.

It looked like the yearling.

Getting over his surprise, Sully told Rae, "Looks like I'm not going to have to go looking for your runaway in the dark after all."

Rae stared, trying to make out the horse's shape. It was really murky out.

"Why did he come back?" Rae cried softly, almost afraid of spooking the yearling.

"I don't think it has anything to do with us," Sully said. "It looks like he just might be showing off for the stallion I rode."

Sully looked around for the rope he'd brought with him. Finding it on the ground, he picked it up, intending on using it the way he'd initially meant to—as a lariat.

But when he turned in the direction of the yearling, he saw that Rae was already walking toward it, talking softly and coaxing the horse to remain still.

She drew closer and closer until she was finally next to the yearling.

Patting its muzzle and still talking softly to the horse, she used the same tone addressing Sully. "Now would be a good time to bring over that lariat, Sully."

It took his a second to realize that she was talking to him. Surprised, Sully picked up the rope again. He caught himself just in time before he started to hurry over to Rae.

Keeping his gait subdued, he crossed slowly over to Rae. When he reached her, he handed her the lariat. She in turn slowly slipped the rope over the horse's head, all the while continuing to talk to the yearling in a quiet, reassuring tone.

"Good boy," she purred against the horse's ear.

Raising her eyes until they met Sully's, she repeated the words. "Good boy."

Hearing her, the corners of Sully's mouth curved in a deep smile, letting Rae know that he understood.

Just as the yearling was secured, the very distinct sound of an approaching sheriff's department vehicle pierced the air.

He had almost forgotten that he'd had Rae call the sheriff, Sully thought.

Looking at her now, he said, "I guess you did get through."

"I said I did," she reminded him. "Reception now is a lot better than it was even five years ago. Ten years ago you were better off beating a drum and trying to communicate that way than trying to reach someone over your cell phone."

Bringing his car to a stop near Rae and Sully, the sheriff looked grim as he got out. His face grew even grimmer when he saw Warren's body.

"Looks like you found your missing wrangler," he commented, squatting down and taking a better look at the mud-caked body. "Any idea what happened to him?" he asked, directing his question at both Sully and Rae.

"Not a clue," Sully answered. "Thought we might have a better idea about that once the medical examiner brings Warren in, washes all this mud off him and does an autopsy. Once we have the cause of death, we might be able to go from there."

Rick rose to his feet and turned toward Sully. "There's one problem with that—we don't have a medical examiner," he told Sully. "The closest one is about fifty miles away, and I've got a feeling that he won't be coming out until sometime tomorrow morning. Possibly later." He saw the surprise on Sully's face. "This is a very quiet town. There's no work for a medical examiner," he explained.

"You can't leave Warren lying out here all night," Rae protested. "The animals will start in on him."

"I've got no intention of leaving him out here," Rick assured her. He looked at the body and said grimly, "I'll put his body in my car." He frowned. "Even wrapped up, that back seat is going to be hell to get clean," he predicted. "You sure neither one of you has any idea how he wound up like this?"

"No," Sully told the sheriff. "I wouldn't have even found him except that I literally stumbled over his body. My horse nearly tripped over the mound of dirt created by someone burying him out here."

Rick slowly circled around the body on the ground as if that would somehow make him think of something. It didn't. He raised his eyes to look at Sully. "I take it you haven't checked for bullet holes or stab wounds."

"We were barely able to dig him up out of the ground," Sully said, including Rae in the effort even though he had done all the work. He'd never been the type to demand the spotlight. "Without a shovel, this mud you have out here isn't exactly compliant, especially when there's rain still coming down."

"It's a wonder you got him out at all," Rick marveled. "Well, we'd better get him into my car if we're going to bring him back to town. We'll put him in the trunk," he decided. "Grab his legs."

Sully went to the dead man's legs while Rae went toward the sheriff's vehicle to open up the trunk. But before Sully bent down to pick up Warren's legs, he suddenly asked the sheriff, "You've got a doctor out here, don't you?"

Rick looked at him uncertainly. "Yeah. Two, as a matter of fact. Why? Are you feeling sick?"

"No. But one of the doctors could do the autopsy," Sully said. "Doctors work on cadavers in medical school, right?"

Rick smiled as he nodded, then looked toward Rae. "Looks like the city boy's right," he said with satisfaction. He was going to get his answers faster than he had reckoned on, Rick thought.

Chapter 12

Dr. Daniel Davenport drove his nine-year-old silver Toyota SUV into the parking area located behind the medical clinic. The area was almost deserted, a rare phenomenon since twelve hours a day—if not more—the clinic was open for business and usually packed with patients. It had been that way ever since Dan had arrived in Forever from New York City and reopened the medical clinic in tribute to his late brother.

Prior to that point, the clinic had been shut down for over thirty years. If anyone had needed or wanted to see a doctor, they had to travel some fifty miles to get to the nearest doctor.

Coming out to reopen the clinic had only been meant as a temporary thing at the time, until he could get someone permanent to come out. But somewhere along the line, it had turned into his life's work—and Dan did it happily.

These days Dan ran the clinic with another doctor, Dr. Alisha Cordell, two nurses and a receptionist who was herself training to become a nurse. The clinic was always busy.

The residents of Forever viewed Dan as their savior and he credited them for having saved his life, because being here gave him a purpose he had never really had before.

Despite the fact that he had a family, also thanks to Forever, Dan always considered himself to be on call, and he never turned anyone away. However, he had to admit he'd really been surprised by the urgency in the sheriff's voice when he'd called.

Getting out of his car now, Dan walked over toward the only other vehicle in the lot.

Because the rain still hadn't entirely abated, the sheriff had remained in his vehicle. Seeing the doctor, he got out now. As did the two people who had accompanied him. They got out of the back seat.

"Thanks for coming out, Doc," Rick said once Dan had reached him.

"Sure."

Dan hadn't realized that anyone else would be coming. He looked now at the other two people with the sheriff. He knew Rae, but he had just made the other man's acquaintance at Murphy's the night of Miss Joan's party. His eyes shifted back to Rick.

"Am I missing something here?" Dan asked.

Rather than answer him, Rick went to the rear of his vehicle and popped open the trunk. Dan followed him, then took a step back, all but colliding with Rae and Sully, who were right behind him.

"Whoa." Dan looked at the sheriff. "You really need to warn a man before springing a sight like that on him." He stared at the muddied body of what apparently was a dead man. All Rick had told him at the time was that it was an emergency and he needed to come as soon as possible. "Who is—*was*," Dan corrected himself, "that?" he asked, nodding at the body.

"That's what's left of John Warren after we dug him out of what we assumed was supposed to be his final resting place," Sully explained. "It was on the north end of the ranch," he added for good measure.

"Miss Joan's ranch?" Dan asked, trying to clarify things.

Rae nodded. "He's been missing since the night of that party at Murphy's."

Dan looked back at the body in the trunk, shaking his head. Given just the moonlight, it was hard to make out the body's features. "How did he wind up like this?" he asked incredulously.

"Well, we were kind of hoping you could tell us," Rick said.

Dan made the obvious leap. "You want me to do an autopsy?"

Rick could hear the reluctance in Dan's voice. "I know it's a lot to ask, but yes, that's what I'm asking you to do," he replied.

Dan scanned the faces of the three people in the

lot with him. "You do realize that I'm not a medical examiner, don't you?" he asked, still having trouble believing all this.

"We know that," Rick replied, "but you are a doctor. The closest medical examiner is fifty miles away, and to be really effective, an autopsy needs to be done as close to the time of death as possible. Warren's already been dead for a few days, maybe longer," he guessed.

Dan sighed, nodding. "I get it. All right, let me open up the clinic." He glanced toward the sheriff. "You and Sully can carry Warren into the back. We can get him cleaned up in the last exam room and then I'll get started. You planning on waiting?" Dan asked just as he was about to open up the front entrance.

"For as long as it takes," Rick answered the doctor grimly.

"Me, too," Sully said, adding his voice to the sheriff's. Everything about this case had him curious, and he wasn't about to check out now. Turning toward Rae, Sully told her, "I'll let you know what the doctor finds out."

"The hell you will," she told him tersely. "I'm going to be right there in the waiting room with you." She saw Rick and Sully exchange looks and put her own interpretation to it. In their minds, they were trying to protect her. "Look, I'm not going anywhere until I get some answers," Rae informed them.

"You heard the lady," Dan said to the others. "The sooner we get this started, the sooner I can have some answers for you. Hopefully," he added. Although Dan was an optimist these days, he was a practical one and didn't allow his optimism to carry him away.

The sheriff and Sully carefully lifted Warren's body out of the trunk and carried the dead man into the clinic. Rae moved ahead of them to hold open the clinic door and then the door to the examination room.

"How long does it take to do one of these things?" Rick asked the other two people in the waiting room with him.

By his count, it had been over an hour and a half now. Restless, he had begun pacing around in circles, growing progressively more restless as the time passed.

"Between two and four hours," Sully answered automatically.

Rick and Rae both looked at him in surprise. The sheriff's question had been more or less rhetorical.

"One of my cousins is an ME," Sully explained.

"Too bad we couldn't have sent him the body," Rae commented.

"Her," Sully corrected. "And this is actually faster. Kristin said they usually have their hands full. Kristin's the medical examiner I mentioned," he explained further.

"I guess we're lucky to be this peaceful," Rick decided, sitting down again on one of the chairs. "Two to four hours, eh?" he repeated. It was obvious that although he was resigned, he wasn't happy about it.

Sully tried to give the man a little hope. "It depends on the condition of the body being autopsied as well as how big the person was and how decomposed."

Rick considered the stipulations Sully had just enumerated. "Well, other than his color once the mud was washed off—and the fact that he was dead—Warren looked to be in pretty good shape," he assessed.

Just then, they heard the door in the rear of the clinic being opened. Dan and Alisha used the third examination room to do minor surgical procedures in lieu of shipping a patient off to the hospital, which was also fifty miles away. This was the first time that an autopsy was being performed in the room.

All three people in the waiting room were on their feet, hurrying toward the rear of the clinic.

Dan met them in the middle. The blue surgical garb he had put on for the procedure had blood on it, and he looked really tired.

"Are you finished with the autopsy?" Rick asked.

"In the interest of brevity," Dan told them, "I just did a preliminary one." He paused to strip off his gloves and remove the mask that was now hanging from about his neck.

"Were you able to determine the cause of death?" Sully asked.

Even with the mud washed off to a greater degree, it was hard for Dan to distinguish what was a wound and what was actually bruises and scratches.

Dan nodded. "There were two knife wounds delivered straight to the heart. As near as I can see, Warren bled out, most likely after whoever did this to him buried him," Dan conjectured. "The poor guy didn't have enough strength to dig himself out of his impromptu grave, much less try to get help."

Envisioning the scene, Rae shivered. But her expression seemed almost stony as she asked the doctor, "Did you find out anything else?"

Dan wearily shook his head. "No, sorry. The actual ME can do a tox screen once you transport the body to the hospital. Maybe it'll produce some more answers."

"You did great, Doc," Rick told the man with enthusiasm. "I know this was a huge imposition. Thanks a lot for coming out and doing this—especially on such short notice."

Dan flashed an even wearier smile. "Sorry I couldn't have been more help," he apologized.

The sheriff saw the look on Rae's face. She looked particularly upset. "What's the matter?"

Rae shook her head. "I still don't know who to notify."

"Maybe there's something in his things that'll tell you," Rick suggested.

That wasn't going to be of any help, she thought. "He took his things with him," she answered.

"I can go back at first light to where we found him." Sully told her. "Maybe Warren's knapsack is there somewhere." He said it to give Rae a sliver of hope, although he strongly doubted that he'd unearth the knapsack.

And then he thought of something and swung around to look at the doctor. "Doc, his fingerprints weren't obliterated, were they?"

Dan looked at the detective, slightly confused. "Are you asking me if they were burned off? No, why would you think that they had been?"

At this point, he wasn't taking anything for granted. "Just checking," Sully answered. He turned toward the sheriff. "We can take his fingerprints and I can forward them to the crime scene investigation lab techs back in Aurora."

"Won't they think you're freelancing?" Rick asked. He was only half kidding.

"My uncle runs the lab's day shift," Sully told him. "I can get him to see if Warren ever worked anyplace before he came here where he would have had to be fingerprinted. If he did, we can match the place to the city where he came from." He saw the dubious look on the sheriff's face. "The database in the department is pretty extensive," he explained.

Rick was beginning to think that the detective had access to endless resources. "Hey, I'm just glad for the help," the sheriff told him.

"Kind of makes you feel like life is passing Forever by, doesn't it?" Rae commented to the man.

"I see it as a tradeoff," Rick answered. "Because along with all that state-of-the-art technology come all the invasive headaches that go with it." He smiled at Rae. "I like things peaceful and quiet myself."

The doctor nodded. "I tend to agree with you, Sheriff. Now, unless you want anything else, let's get a copy of those prints to send out and then I'm going to lock this clinic up—for another six hours before patients start turning up at the door," he told the others with a resigned sigh.

"Let me go to my office so I can get an inkpad and paper for you," the sheriff told Dan. "We might as well keep this as official as possible," he added as he headed toward the front entrance.

Sully started to take a seat in order to wait for the sheriff's return. Rae, he noticed, was going toward the rear of the clinic. With a suppressed sigh, he rose to his feet again.

Dan realized that Rae was behind him and he stopped walking. "Do you need something, Rae?"

"No, but I thought you might need some help cleaning up in the back." She saw the puzzled look on his face and said, "I mean, you did just do an autopsy back there, right?"

"Cleaning off the mud on his body made more of a mess than the autopsy did," Dan assured her.

"All right, then I'll clean up the mud," she volunteered.

Anyone else would have been more than willing to sit this out. "Are you sure you want to do this?" Dan asked her.

"Want to?" she repeated. "No. But I like being useful. I'm sure you didn't want to leave your nice, cozy home to come in and cut up a dead body, especially since you needed to clean it up first."

Dan could see that arguing with her was definitely an exercise in futility.

"Okay," he said, giving in. "Come this way."

"Got room for one more?" Sully asked, catching up to them after first attempting to argue himself out of doing this. When Dan looked at him quizzically, Sully told the doctor, "Well, it's not like I've got something else to do."

"This is going to go down as one of the strangest nights I've ever spent in Forever," Dan told them as he led the way to the last exam room.

He pushed open the door again. He'd pulled it shut out of habit when he'd left the room.

Aside from several towels that were all bunched up on the floor in one corner, towels that Dan had used on the body when he was cleaning off the mud, the room appeared to be fairly clean.

However, fairly clean wasn't good enough. Rae knew that the room had to be kept sterile from patient to patient.

"You want me to boil something or pour boiling water on it to sterilize it?" she asked Dan, not knowing exactly what sort of procedure he followed.

Dan looked as if he was having trouble trying not to laugh, but he managed to keep a straight face since he didn't want to offend her.

"Just put those towels into the hamper and wipe down the exam table with some alcohol." He pointed toward a generic opaque bottle over on the counter beneath a cabinet.

"Anything else, Doc?" Sully asked, looking around the rectangular room.

"Not unless you can think of something," Dan

said. Hearing a noise coming from the front of the clinic, Dan glanced in that direction. "Hopefully that's the sheriff and not a patient looking to be first in line when we officially open our doors."

Sully had no frame of reference for the kind of foot traffic the doctor was talking about.

"Are you always busy?" he asked.

"Always," Dan told him, and then he smiled. "And I wouldn't have it any other way. I like making a difference," he confided. "To be honest with you, this feels a lot better than having the kind of practice where I make enough money to buy a new Ferrari every two years. That, by the way, was the kind of doctor I *thought* I was going to be—until I came out here and realized what being a doctor really meant."

"Why *did* you come out here?" Sully asked the former New York doctor just as the sheriff walked into the exam room.

"Long story," Dan answered. "Maybe I'll tell it to you if you stick around here long enough," he added, crossing the room to meet the sheriff.

The latter produced a large inkpad and regulation paper to collect Warren's fingerprints and offered it to the visiting detective.

"Do you want to do the honors?" the sheriff asked Sully.

"This is still your jurisdiction, Sheriff," he told the sheriff. "I wouldn't want to step on your toes or anything."

Rae rolled her eyes. "If the two of you will stop being so nauseatingly polite," she said to Sully and the sheriff, "I think Doc is really ready to lock up and go home."

But Dan had another thought as Rick carefully collected the dead man's fingerprints.

"What about the body?" he asked, looking at the man he had just put back together and sewn up. The stitched-up Y incision appeared particularly vivid on the dead wrangler's chest.

Rick wasn't following his friend's meaning. "What about it?"

"Do you want to leave him here like this until morning?" Dan asked the sheriff. "Or do you want to store him somewhere?"

Rick knew what the doctor was alluding to. That as outlandish as it sounded, the body might be stolen. He really doubted that anyone would break into the clinic for that sole purpose, but then he wouldn't have thought anyone would have stabbed someone to death in his town, either. For the time being, there were no norms to cling to.

"Good point," Rick agreed.

But before the sheriff could offer up a course of action regarding overseeing the body until morning arrived, Sully said, "I'll stay with the body."

Sully's eyes swept over the other three people in the room and he added, "Unless there are any objections, of course."

Chapter 13

"I don't have any objection," Rae said, speaking up. "But if anyone should stay here with the body, it should be me," she told Sully as well as the sheriff. "Warren worked for me. I owe this to him," she said. She gave no indication that she was about to be dissuaded.

Sully's eyes met hers. She saw pity there, and it annoyed her.

"Don't you have a ranch to run?" he asked.

She looked somewhat grim as she considered the question. "At this point, I'm really not sure if I do or not."

"What are you talking about?" the sheriff asked.

Her expression only grew more somber. "I'm supposed to keep the ranch running smoothly, and I think that this definitely qualifies as not smoothly," she said, looking over at the form lying on the table beneath the sheet Dan had placed over him.

"You didn't kill Warren," Sully pointed out.

"No, but I also didn't keep him from running off and consequently having this happen to him." Rae gestured toward the table.

"I'll tell Miss Joan about finding Warren in the morning," Rick told her kindly. "No point in waking her with this news now."

It would have been easier that way, Rae thought and part of her was very tempted just to let the sheriff take over as he'd volunteered. She didn't look forward to seeing the look of disappointment in her benefactress's eyes. But she lived up to her responsibilities, and telling Miss Joan about Warren getting killed was all part of that.

"Thank you, Sheriff, but no, I have to be the one to tell her," Rae said.

Rick didn't look overly happy about her decision—this was his town and he felt responsible for it—but he understood the position she was taking.

"If you change your mind, Rae, you know where to find me."

Rather than saying anything, Rae merely nodded. She waited until both the sheriff and the doctor left the clinic. The quiet that ensued once they were gone was jarring.

Looking at the remaining person with her, she told Sully, "You know you don't have to stay."

The look on his face said that she wasn't about to

push him out. "I'm not staying because I have to," he told her.

She sighed. "Why are you staying, then?" she asked.

Sully held up one finger. "I'm the one who found him, and," he continued, raising a second finger, "I figure you could use the company."

She didn't know if he was being kind or patronizing. "This isn't a sleepover, Cavanaugh," Rae pointed out.

"I wasn't intending on sleeping," he informed her, the corners of his mouth curving just the slightest bit, as if he was privately sharing some humorous anecdote with himself.

Her eyes narrowed just a little. "Nothing else is going to happen, either," she informed him just in case he was getting any ideas about the two of them being together in close quarters with no one else around to chaperone them.

Sully looked totally unfazed. "Good to know," he replied.

Confused and frustrated, Rae blew out a breath. "You know, you are a very complicated man, Sully Cavanaugh," she accused.

"On the contrary, I'm a very simple man. If I have a job to do, I keep at it until it's done. And then I just kick back and relax. Pretty much like most people," he concluded.

"You are *not* like most people," Rae informed him with finality.

They were still out in the waiting room. It was easier to talk out here than it was with a deceased body nearby. Another smile tugged at the corners of Sully's mouth.

"Why, Rachel Mulcahy, is that a compliment?" he asked, his hand covering his heart.

She shot down his lighthearted humor. "No, that wasn't a compliment, and don't call me Rachel. My name is Rae," she insisted.

She was trying to divest herself of all trace of softness, he thought. But it was still visible. "Rachel is prettier."

Did he think she cared what he thought? "The name is Rae," she repeated with more feeling.

"Tough, able," he said, analyzing the name. "Is that what you're going for?"

For two cents, she would have read him the riot act. But for some reason, she felt compelled to actually answer Sully's question. "Not that it's any business of yours, but out here I have to exhibit those qualities above all else."

"I think we'd both agree that life was rougher in biblical times." Before she could ask him why he was suddenly babbling about biblical times, Sully answered her unspoken question. "In the Bible, it said that Jacob toiled seven years in order to marry Rachel, only to be tricked into marrying her older sister. That would have been pretty daunting for another couple. But he persisted—and so did Rachel. And after toiling another seven years for her, they were finally married. By waiting for him, Rachel proved to be just as strong and tough as he was."

She frowned. "Fascinating, Cavanaugh, and very

educational. But I still like the name Rae. My dad used to call me Rae. I know it was because he wanted a boy." There was no malice in her voice, no indication that realizing that fact hurt her. "But it didn't matter," she insisted. "I *like* the name Rae."

Listening, Sully drew his own conclusion. "A rose by any other name…" His voice trailed off.

Her eyebrows drew together in a quizzical expression. "What are you talking about?" she asked.

Sully smiled. "That's a lesson for another day. It doesn't matter," he said good-naturedly. "Rae's a nice name." Changing the subject, he said, "Why don't you stretch out on one of the sofas? I'll keep watch over our stationary friend back there." He nodded toward the rear of the clinic. "He's not about to go anywhere, anyway."

"I don't think the sheriff was worried about that," she told Sully. And then she grew just a little quieter and serious. "You don't think whoever killed him is going to try to make off with the body, do you?" It sounded impossible, but then, twenty-four hours ago the idea of a murder in Forever seemed impossible.

"Not unless Warren swallowed something that would give away his killer's identity." The moment he said the words, Sully saw an uncertain look come over Rae's face. "Look, Forever's different from anything I'm used to, I'll grant you that. But I really doubt that Warren has anything inside him that would tell us who his killer was."

"You're right," Rae agreed, but she didn't sound convinced.

"I'll ask the doc in the morning if there was anything out of the ordinary about Warren's autopsy that he didn't mention—just in case," Sully promised.

Rae murmured, "Thanks," saying the word as if it was difficult for her to voluntarily utter it.

"So, why don't you stretch out like I said?" he asked, nodding at the closest sofa.

"I'm exhausted," she admitted, "but there's no way I'm going to get any sleep, not while I'm trying to figure out just how I'm going to tell Miss Joan about this." She saw him opening his mouth and cut him off. "And don't tell me that I should let the sheriff handle it. That's not his job."

"Actually," Sully contradicted, "notifying next of kin and other interested parties about someone's death *is* his job."

Hearing him mention next of kin reminded her of something else she still had to do. "And that's another thing—I need to find out if Warren even *had* any next of kin."

Her words brought back the response he'd given her earlier. He'd promised that he intended to look into that for her.

"Right," Sully said. Rae watched the detective take out his cell phone and press his thumb against the lower part of the screen. "Why don't I get started on that?"

"Now?" Rae asked incredulously. She looked at her watch. "It's two thirty in the morning."

"It's even earlier than that in Aurora," he told her as he began to type in a text to his cousin. "But I want Valri to see this first thing in the morning, before she gets in."

"Valri?" Rae repeated. She was certain that he hadn't mentioned the name to her before.

Sully nodded without looking up from the cell screen. "My cousin."

"The medical examiner?" she asked, trying to keep things straight.

He glanced up. "That's another cousin," he told her. "This one is a computer wizard, and she can access databases that the average person hasn't even thought of yet." He took a picture of the fingerprints that had been lifted from the deceased, sending them along with the text message he'd just written.

Finished, Sully began to head toward the last exam room.

Rae was right behind him. "Now what are you doing?" she asked.

"I'm going to take a couple of close-ups of those stab wounds in Warren's chest and send them to Kristin to see if she notices anything unusual about them," Sully explained.

"Kristin." She was having trouble keeping the names straight. "And that would be the medical examiner?"

He was preoccupied and muttered, "Yes."

Rae wanted to ask more questions. But she waited as Sully moved the sheet back and took several photographs of the entry wounds on the dead man's chest.

Warren looked progressively worse each time

she looked at him, Rae thought. She could feel her stomach threatening to turn over and send up her last meal.

In addition to keeping her food down, she was having trouble keeping her guilt from overwhelming her.

She kept quiet until she thought Sully was finished. "Anyone else you want to send a photo array off to?" she asked.

She was being sarcastic, but he answered her seriously.

"My uncle Sean," he said as the thought occurred to him. "I'll ask the doc about processing Warren's DNA in the morning and I can send that to Uncle Sean," he said, thinking out loud.

"Why would you want to collect Warren's DNA?" she asked. "We already have his name."

"Just a hunch," he answered vaguely.

Rae looked at him more closely, second-guessing what was going through his head. "You don't think John Warren's his real name, do you?"

"It probably is," he said, "but given what you said about not knowing anything about his background, you can't really rule out anything at this point." He carefully replaced the sheet over the man's body. "If he'd been born and raised here, that would be another story."

"Yes, it would be," she said, her mind straying. She couldn't think about Warren right now. Not until she could find out who killed him and why. Instead, she forced herself to focus on the immediate situation and the man she was sharing space with. "Just how many people on the police force are you related to, Cavanaugh?"

"At times, too many to keep straight," he readily confessed.

She looked at him. "You make it sound like a bad thing."

"At times it can get pretty overwhelming," he admitted.

He missed them now, Sully thought, and that was a good feeling. It was comforting to know that there was always someone who had his back, no matter what happened.

"Overwhelmed by relatives," Rae said, trying to relate to that situation. But she couldn't begin to fathom something like that. She shook her head. "Can't say I know what that's like. I've been on my own since I was fifteen."

"What about Miss Joan?" he reminded her.

"Miss Joan looked out for me when I was fifteen," she admitted, "but she's not a relative."

"It doesn't take blood to make a family," he told her. "All it takes is caring."

Her mouth twisted, lost between a semi-smile and a spate of emotion that left unchecked was liable to bring on tears.

Trying to block those emotions, she flippantly told him, "You missed your calling, Cavanaugh. All these years you could have been writing greeting cards."

Rather than get annoyed, Sully took her comment

in stride. "That might be something to fall back on," he said agreeably.

"Think they'll get back to you?" she asked. When he looked at her, obviously waiting for more input, she elaborated, "The medical examiner and the computer wizard you texted. Do you think they'll get back to you any time soon?"

"With any luck, I'll hear from them first thing in the morning." He smiled fondly as he thought of Valri. "Val looks as if she's a very quiet, soft-spoken, laid-back young woman who loves technology, but she has this incredibly competitive streak."

Rae didn't understand his point. "Who is she competing with?"

He grinned. "Herself. She's always pitting herself against her last best time, wanting to be faster, more thorough than she was the last time."

That sounded pretty exhausting, Rae thought. "And the medical examiner?"

The medical examiner was actually married to his cousin Malloy, but he left that little piece of information out for now. No sense in confusing Rae with a barrage of names, he thought.

"Kristin just doesn't like leaving any questions unanswered," Sully told her.

"And you're related to these two people?" Rae asked, attempting to organize the people, their names and fields of expertise in her mind.

"To them and to a lot more like them," Sully answered her.

"And these 'lot more like them,' are they all in law

enforcement?" she asked, having trouble wrapping her mind around a phenomenon like that.

"In one form or another, yes, they are," Sully answered.

"And what do you do, exactly?" she asked.

He merely smiled and said, "My part."

Modest, she thought and laughed softly. "Well, that settles it," Rae declared as if she had just reached a decision after a prolonged debate. "In my next life, I'm coming back as you."

Sully laughed then, the deep, warm sound resonating around the room and seeming to encompass most of the clinic.

"Why are you laughing?" Rae asked. Her comment might have been unorthodox, but she didn't think she said anything particularly amusing. "What's so funny, Cavanaugh?"

"Because you coming back as me would be a terrible, terrible waste," he told her.

Her eyebrows drew together. "And why is that?"

"Because," Sully explained, his eyes sweeping over her in a way that felt incredibly intimate to Rae. She felt everything tightening within her, as if poised for something—except that she didn't really know what.

"Because?" she questioned, the lone word hanging out in space, teasing her.

"Because," he told her in a lowered voice, "you're perfect just the way you are."

"No, I'm not," she insisted, dismissing his assessment. She felt that there was nothing perfect about her.

The description, *perfect*, belonged to beautiful women who sat jauntily back against a wall of pillows, looking as if they belonged on the cover of exclusive fashion magazine. The word wasn't used to describe to a woman who had rough hands and spent her waking hours working hard.

"Yes," Sully told her, his voice soft, low. "You are." And then, for once in his life, he didn't think—he just reacted and went with an overpowering feeling that had been eating away at him ever since he had first laid eyes on Rae. Sully cupped her face between his hands and kissed her.

Chapter 14

Rae could feel herself responding to Sully's kiss half a second before his lips touched hers. Her skin warmed in anticipation as her heart began to beat faster and faster. She told herself that she was over-reacting, that what was happening was just a matter of one set of lips on another.

Nothing more than skin on skin.

There was absolutely no reason for her to feel as if there was a party going on inside her, especially in view of the fact that there was a dead body lying several rooms away.

It didn't matter.

Logic didn't matter.

Rae felt as if she was a lone flower struggling to

bloom in the desert, desperate for that one nourishing drop of water.

That's what this kiss was to her.

As Rae rose up higher on her toes, absorbing the effects of this pulse-quickening kiss, she felt Sully's strong arms slip down to her waist, holding her to him.

She surrendered herself up to the sensation, glorying in the powerful burst of desire that seemed to pour through her entire body.

A level of desire she had never experienced before captured her.

Just as she felt herself succumbing, Sully drew back from her.

"Sorry," he murmured. "I couldn't help myself."

She could literally hear her heart hammering in her ears. She would have given in to him, to this desire, if he had just pushed a little.

But he hadn't.

And he seemed to regret what had almost happened.

Rae fought hard to save face. "Don't let it happen again," Rae warned, her voice verging on sheer breathlessness.

His eyes held hers as he told her, "I won't."

But they both knew that it would happen again. And the next time it did, it wouldn't end with Sully drawing back away from her. Nor, she knew, would she even *want* him to draw back.

But for now, she needed to gather herself together and focus on the task at hand: telling Miss Joan what had happened to the last man she had sent to the ranch before Sully arrived—and joining forces with the sheriff and Sully to find the man's killer.

"The offer to come with you still stands," Sully told her when morning finally arrived.

They had both remained at the clinic the entire night, guarding Warren's body. Hearing about it, the sheriff's wife had taken pity on Sully and Rae and sent over clean clothing for them, The sheriff returned to take over at first light, saying he was staying with the body until the medical examiner from the next town arrived to do an even more thorough autopsy.

Relieved of their impromptu duty by the sheriff, she and Sully were free to go about their business. For Rae, that meant that she was going to deliver the news about Warren's murder to Miss Joan.

"I already told you," Rae said to the detective, "I don't need to have my hand held."

"I know," Sully answered. "But maybe I just want to."

There was that smile again, she thought, the one that seemed to just slip in under her skin like a perfect incision delivered by the tip of a razor-sharp scalpel. She could actually *feel* it leaving its mark.

"All right," she said, giving in, "you want to come? Come."

The smile morphed into a grin. "Since you asked so nicely... I'm kidding," Sully told her quickly when he saw lightning forming in her eyes. "You really need to lighten up a little, Mulcahy."

Leaving the clinic, she didn't see it that way. "This is a serious situation," she insisted.

"No one's arguing that," Sully said, following her down the front steps. They headed toward Miss Joan's diner. "But I learned a long time ago that a sense of humor can see you through a lot. If you don't laugh, you cry," he told her simply. "And crying never helped anything."

Every step she took toward Miss Joan's felt as if her legs were turning into lead. Listening to these mindless adages just seemed to make everything worse.

"Do you just come up with these things," she asked him, "or are they sewn on some dish towel somewhere for your personal use?"

He grinned. "They're right next to those greeting cards we talked about," he told her.

She made a dismissive noise that sounded more like a muffled groan but said nothing intelligible to Sully in response.

Reaching the diner, he opened the door for her and held it as Rae walked in ahead of him.

She held her breath as she looked around.

The diner was fairly empty at this hour, having already seen its first wave of activity, earlier risers who needed to be on the job before eight. There was only one waitress on duty at this time, and she was busy clearing off the last of the tables.

Miss Joan was where she usually was, behind

the counter. Her back was to the door and she was refilling the two giant side-by-side urns with fresh coffee. The first wave of customers had consumed almost all of the coffee.

Sensing their presence, Miss Joan said, "Be with you in a minute," as she poured the last of the water into the urns. The low rumble let her and anyone else in the immediate area know that the coffee was beginning to brew.

Drying off her hands on her apron, Miss Joan turned around to face them. She didn't look surprised, but then, her expression rarely gave anything away.

"Both of you," she commented. "What's up?"

"What makes you think something's up?" Sully asked her. He was curious just how acute the woman's thought process was. Ordinarily, anyone else would have just said hello.

"Don't insult me, boy," Miss Joan told him. "The breakfast here is good, but Rae's capable of making one every bit as good. She learned everything she knows about cooking working here next to Angel— even if she claims not to like to cook." Her sharp hazel eyes swept over both of them, searching for any telltale signs of a clue. "Now have a seat. I'll pour you a couple of cups of freshly brewed coffee and you can tell me why you're here."

It wasn't a suggestion.

Rae couldn't wait for the coffee. She needed to get this off her chest and out in the open before it smothered her.

"John Warren isn't missing anymore."

Miss Joan placed one cup of black coffee in front of Rae and a second one in front of Sully. The creamer was in a polished container on the counter between them. "He turned up."

It wasn't exactly a question the way she said it, but Rae took it to be. She forced herself to breathe normally.

"In a manner of speaking," she answered.

"And just what manner is that?" Miss Joan asked.

It seemed to Sully that the woman seemed amazingly calm as she went about accumulating information. His gut told him that she wasn't going to be surprised with what Rae was about to tell her. The woman was unique, he thought, and he was beginning to see why his uncle liked her so much.

"One of the yearlings took off yesterday, spooked by the storm. Sully went looking for it and his horse stumbled over this mound of dirt," Rae said, trying to choose her words carefully.

Miss Joan cut to the chase. "How long was Warren buried?"

Stunned, Rae stared at the older woman, momentarily speechless. "You know?"

"That's where this story's headed, isn't it?" Miss Joan asked the question like someone who already knew the answer. "Given that I don't have a fondness for long, convoluted tales, that has to be the reason in your mind why you're telling me all this."

Unable to remain silent any longer, Sully spoke up. "We don't know how long he was there."

Miss Joan nodded. "I figured as much. Rae would have led with that if you did," she said confidently. Her eyes swept over them slowly. "Do either of you have any idea who might have done this to him?"

"No," Sully said, answering for both of them. "Warren seemed like a nice guy who kept mostly to himself."

Rae seconded that, adding, "Everyone seemed to like him except for Rawlings." She frowned slightly. "But Rawlings really doesn't seem to like anyone."

Taking this in, Miss Joan nodded. "Much as it pains me to admit it, I might have made the wrong call about that man," she said, clearly referring to Rawlings. "I'll give him to the end of the month to get his act together." She slanted a look toward Rae, pinning her in place. "I want weekly progress reports on him from you."

"Yes, Miss Joan," Rae said dutifully.

"As for Warren," Miss Joan continued, "did he confide in either one of you about where he came from or if he had any family anywhere?" she asked.

Both Sully and Rae shook their heads.

"I just asked the sheriff about getting a sample of Warren's DNA," Sully told the woman. "I thought I'd ask someone back at the police department in Aurora if they could track down any kind of personal information on Warren."

Rae noticed that Miss Joan didn't look surprised that Sully was doing this. Instead, she just took the information in stride. It was obvious that she approved of his efforts.

"Good. And," she added with finality, "if you can't find anyone, once Warren's body is released, I'll take care of his funeral costs."

She said it with the same kind of emphasis she would have given to volunteering to pick up a vacationing person's mail. No fanfare, no undo attention, just a simple fact of life.

Not for the first time Rae couldn't help thinking how really selfless the woman was beneath all of her sharp words and her bluster.

Miss Joan looked the two people in front of her carefully. "Have you two eaten yet today?" she asked them suddenly.

"No," Rae answered for both of them. "But we need to get back. I left Rawlings in charge, and heaven only knows what I'm going to find there by the time we get back."

Miss Joan wasn't impressed by Rae's fears. "The ranch'll keep for another hour," the woman told her. "You're having breakfast."

It wasn't a question—it was an order, one that was not to be questioned.

"And while you're waiting on that DNA information to come back," Miss Joan told them after placing an order for two breakfast specials with everything with the short-order cook in the back, "I'll ask around if anyone knows anything about Warren that might not have come to light before."

"You know," Sully told the woman, "if you ever decide to leave the diner and Forever, you should think about coming out to Aurora. You would be a real asset to the police department."

Miss Joan shook her head. "No, thanks. You city people are much too fast for me."

There was no way that Sully believed that or thought that Miss Joan actually believed it. But he knew enough not to laugh. "Nobody could even come close to you, Miss Joan."

She merely smiled at the compliment.

They had just finished eating and looked as if they were about to leave the diner. "Since you're going to be shorthanded while you two are caught up in this investigation, I called Clint Washburn while you were enjoying Juan's efforts with breakfast. I asked Clint if he'd send over one of his men to the J-H Ranch to help out for a few days."

Miss Joan paused. It was a foregone conclusion that Clint hadn't turned her down.

And he hadn't.

"He's sending his brother Roy, which means that when you two get back to the ranch, you can get some sleep." Her eyes narrowed as she shifted them from one fact to the other. "You both look as if you could use it."

Sully grinned at the woman, discounting the assessment and accompanying suggestion. "I'm just getting my second wind, Miss Joan," he told her. Then, turning toward Rae, he said, "But you could use some."

Rae instantly pulled back her shoulders, looking every bit like someone who was bracing for a fight.

"I'm just fine," she ground out between her teeth.

Clearing away their plates, Miss Joan just shook her head. "Never could tell that girl anything," she told Sully.

Sully merely smiled, sharing the moment with Miss Joan. But he said nothing. He had no desire to set Rae off.

His cell phone vibrated just as they walked out of the diner. He pulled it out as he went down the last steps. Reading what was texted, he told Rae, "Looks like Valri has some information for us."

Rae found it hard to believe. "Seriously? Already?" she asked.

He scrolled to the end of the message. "I told you she was fast."

"Apparently," Rae said under her breath. "Well, what does she say?"

But Sully didn't answer her. The text on his phone kept updating. He continued reading the additional texts that his cousin was sending. Finished, he re-read all of the texts again.

"What is it?" Rae repeated. She shifted in order to be able to read the cell screen he was holding. "Don't play games with me, Cavanaugh," she warned. "I'm not tired, but I'm short on patience."

"No games," Sully protested. He raised his eyes to hers. "Whoever that wrangler we found actually was, his name wasn't John Warren."

She didn't understand what he was telling her.

Was he saying that it was a case of mistaken identity on their part?

"You mean we didn't find Warren, we found someone else?" It didn't seem possible. The man Sully had pulled out of the muddy grave certainly *looked* like the man who had worked on the ranch for the last two months. "How's that possible?"

Sully looked around to see if they were alone. He didn't want this to get around until he had a chance to tell the sheriff.

But there was no one nearby, so he started to explain the circumstances to Rae.

"We found John Warren all right—except he wasn't John Warren. He was really someone else. John Warren was his alias. According to what Valri found when she ran the fingerprints I sent her, the guy's name was Jefferson Wynters. Valri is forwarding this information—as well as anything else she finds—to me via my laptop. I need to go back to the ranch so I can access it."

This was all news to her. "You brought a laptop?" she questioned. "I thought you wanted to get away from all that."

He'd thrown the laptop in as an afterthought. Now he was glad that he did. "I packed it just in case when I left. I guess it was lucky I did," he commented.

She wasn't going to say it, but she agreed with him—at least on that.

"Did Valri say anything else about this Jefferson Wynters?" she asked. "Like if she found out if he has any next of kin? And if she did, did she say where I can find them?"

"Not that I can see so far," he answered. He'd scrolled down to the bottom, and there was no mention of any family. And then his phone vibrated again, indicating that another message was coming in. "Hold it."

"What is it?" she asked.

Sully scanned the message. "Valri says that Wynters was wanted by the police for questioning."

Rae thought of the mild-mannered, inept man who had been posing as a wrangler all this time. This seemed incredible. "Questioning about what?"

Sully went on reading as they walked over to her vehicle—the sheriff had had one of his deputies drive it into town, thinking she'd want to be able to drive herself and Sully back to the ranch.

Sully gave her the news as he read it. "Apparently, the firm he was working for just before he disappeared reported that a lot of money had gone missing. The manager thought that Warren—Wynters—might have had something to do with it," he said just as they reached her truck.

He kept the phone open as he got into the vehicle.

Rae climbed in on her side. This whole thing was beginning to sound more and more unreal to her.

"What do they mean by a lot of money?" she asked. "Does it say how much went missing?"

Sully continued to scroll as his cousin sent more information. "Valri said she was emailing me all the details, but according to this last piece she's just texted," he said as he read, "it was—"

Sully abruptly stopped talking. His mouth dropped open as an amount appeared on the screen.

About to start the truck, she looked at him. "How much?"

"This can't be right," he murmured, still looking at his phone.

"How much?" Rae repeated. She had always hated not knowing things, and having him draw this out just underscored that for her. "Damn it, Sully, how much was Warren—Wynters," she corrected, "supposed to have made off with?"

"According to this, he stole over half a million dollars."

She stared at Sully in disbelief. "That's not possible."

The text terminated and he slipped the phone back into his pocket. "Whoever killed him obviously thought it was."

Chapter 15

"Why are you stopping?" Sully asked.

He'd assumed that they were going to drive to the ranch, but instead, Rae had turned her truck in the opposite direction. She'd then driven the short distance to the sheriff's office and now pulled up in front of it.

Sully looked at her quizzically. "I thought we were going to the ranch."

"You said you want to go to the ranch to get your laptop," she said, opening the door on her side. "Well, you can access your email account at the sheriff's office." A tolerant smile curved her mouth as she got out. "We're not as backward as you think, and the sheriff does need to hear about this," Rae reminded him.

He realized that he might have offended her when he said he needed to get his laptop to connect to the Aurora police department, but he hadn't meant to. What he was guilty of was tunnel vision, because he was used to doing things a certain way.

Rather than bother wasting time explaining himself, Sully got out of the truck on his side and told her, "Lead the way."

Without another word, she quickly went up the front steps and then went straight to the sheriff's inner office.

Rick looked surprised to see them when they walked in.

"I thought you two would be on your way back to the ranch to get some well-deserved sleep. Something wrong with your truck?" he asked, leaping to the first reason he could think of that would bring them to his office. "Gabe said it made a strange sound when he put it into Park."

"It always makes a strange noise," she told him. "No, this is about some information that we found out about Warren."

Beckoning them inside, he looked from one to the other. "What about Warren?" Rick asked.

Rae looked toward Sully, indicating that the news should come from him since, ultimately, it was his to give. "He's not Warren," Sully told the sheriff.

Confusion creased the sheriff's forehead. "How's that again?"

"Can I have access to one of your computers?" Sully asked him. "I'd like to download my email. I can explain all this a lot better once I can have it all in front of me."

Rick didn't hesitate. He moved back from his desk and gestured toward the desktop computer that he usually kept pushed over to one side.

"Have at it," he told Sully.

Sitting down, Sully started typing. Pulling up the site he was looking for, he inputted his user name and password. Instantly another screen opened up. Within a few moments, Sully's fingers were flying across the keyboard, pulling up lines upon lines of data.

Watching him, Rick marveled, "You type a hell of a lot faster than I do."

"I've probably had more practice," Sully answered. With more information in front of him now, he turned toward the sheriff. "Okay, the man everyone here knew as John Warren was actually Jefferson Wynters. His fingerprints are on file in a national database. Seems that being fingerprinted is required for more and more employees these days, and that includes accountants for firms overseeing the regulations for assisted-living facilities."

"So you're telling me that this Warren-Wynters was an accountant?" Rick asked.

Sully nodded. "According to this information that was just sent to me this morning by one of my cousins, he was."

"An accountant," Rick repeated, stunned. He looked as if he was rolling the word over in his head as he tried to comprehend what was going on. "Yeah,

I suppose that makes more sense. The guy acted more like an accountant than a wrangler." Which brought him to the next question. "So what was he doing here, posing as a ranch hand?"

"My guess would be that he was hiding," Sully said. He scanned the screen to see if there was anything more coming in, but for now there wasn't. "Wynters probably thought that no one would think to look for him working on a horse ranch."

"That stands to reason. It wasn't like he was any good at it. According to what I heard, the guy was pretty inept. But hiding?" Rick questioned as the word Sully had used sank in. "From what?"

This was what was called burying the lead, Sully thought, but it was better to offer the information slowly. He was surprised that Rae had indulged him and kept quiet while he filled the sheriff in.

"Apparently whoever he stole over half a million dollars from." Sully watched the sheriff's face as he divulged that piece of information.

"Wait, back up," Rick ordered, certain that he had heard wrong. "What?"

Sully went into detail. "Wynters was wanted for questioning about half a million dollars that went missing from the company he worked for. The thought was that he embezzled it. When he took off, the likelihood that he was guilty increased tenfold and he became their chief suspect. However," he concluded, "no charges were officially brought against him. Currently the police are still looking for him back in Arizona."

Sully hadn't mentioned another state before. "This happened in Arizona?" Rae asked.

Sully nodded, then specified, "Prescott."

"I've got a question," Rae told him. "Where's the money now?"

Rick took a stab at the answer. "My guess is that whoever killed him has it."

"Or," Sully said, offering another version, "the person killed Wynters because he wouldn't tell him where he—Wynters—had hidden the money."

Rick frowned. He didn't like where this was going. "You realize you just said that the whole town is now under suspicion for this man's murder." He shook his head. "I grew up here. I *know* these people. Some of them are hotheads and can lose their temper, but murder? I don't think so."

Sully wasn't about to argue with the sheriff. He needed the man's goodwill. So for now, he offered a compromise.

"Why don't we start by questioning the people who were at Miss Joan's party, asking them if they saw anything suspicious. We'll go from there," Sully suggested.

"You mean like asking them if anyone saw Warren leaving with someone," Rae clarified.

He'd almost forgotten she was there, Sully thought. He glanced at her now. "Right. Like that. We could—"

"This is still my town, Sully," the sheriff said. He wasn't being territorial—he just felt that the residents would respond better to him than someone they didn't know, as well. "I should do the questioning."

Sully had no problem with that. He just wanted answers. "You're absolutely right. Sorry, I didn't mean to overstep any line," he said, getting up from the desk. "Force of habit."

"Well, in this case I'm glad for any help you can offer," the sheriff admitted. "Robbery on this scale isn't exactly what I'm used to. Throw in murder and I don't mind saying that I'm in over my head."

"No shame in asking for help, Sheriff," Sully told the other man. "I do it all the time."

"You did it last night," Rae reminded Sully. When Rick looked at her, a bemused expression on his face, she realized how what she'd just said had to sound to a third party. She could feel color rising up her cheeks. "When you sent those texts to your two cousins, asking them to check out Warren's fingerprints and the stab wounds in his chest," she quickly added.

She could see that the amusement on the two men's faces didn't abate. She pressed her lips together and stopped talking.

"Right," Sully agreed amiably, although she could see the smile in his eyes. "See, Sheriff? No shame in asking."

Rick pressed on. "There were a lot of people at that party," he commented. "It's going to take a while to question all of them."

"Well, then, we'd better get started with it," Rae said.

Sully glossed over the fact that Rae had said *we*

and said to the sheriff, "They're going to want to know why we're asking if they saw Warren leaving and with who, if anyone," he speculated. "For now, we should just tell everyone that Warren's body was found on the north end of Miss Joan's ranch. They don't have to know that he was murdered—or that he stole over a half a million dollars."

"Allegedly," the sheriff interjected, wanting to keep all the facts straight.

Sully inclined his head. Keeping the questioning low-key was better suited to maintaining a calm situation. "Allegedly," he echoed.

"What about my deputies?" Rick asked the other man. "I don't want to keep them in the dark. I have to tell them the truth."

"Do you trust them?" Sully asked before he answered.

Rick never hesitated. His answer was immediate. "Each and every one of them with my life," he swore.

That was all Sully wanted to hear. "Then tell them," he advised.

"That'll make six of us," Rae told the two men. "How do you want to split this up?" she asked. "We each question an equal amount of people?"

Rick and Sully exchanged looks. "I wasn't planning on having you take part in the questioning—" Sully got no further in his answer.

"The man worked for me," Rae informed him in a steely voice that left no room for argument. "I never picked up on any of this. That's on me. And then someone killed him. Whether or not he stole that money doesn't change the fact that someone stabbed that man to death. No one deserves to have that happen to them," she insisted. She stood between the two men, a small, immovable force who was not about to be dismissed. "I intend to see this through and find out who killed him."

Silence ensued for a very long moment. And then Rick smiled as he looked toward Sully. "You heard the lady, Cavanaugh."

"She's not part of law enforcement," Sully maintained. "Whoever stabbed Warren isn't playing games." His eyes pinned her in place—or so he thought. "You could get hurt," he argued. "Or—"

Rae turned away from Sully as if he hadn't said a word. Instead, she turned toward the sheriff and looked at him. "Deputize me."

"You can't do that," Sully protested.

She raised her head, tossing her hair with an air of defiance. "Yes, he can. Sheriff?"

Rick opened his middle drawer. As Sully watched, the he took out a badge and held it in his left hand. "Raise your right hand," he told Rae.

Rae did as she was told, and Rick proceeded to swear her in as a temporary deputy sheriff.

When Rick finished with the oath and Rae dropped her right hand, he looked at Sully. "She goes with you," he ordered.

"That's defeating the purpose," Rae complained. "Having me there is supposed to help divide up the number of residents each of us question. If I have to go with him, I'm just rubber-stamping Cavanaugh."

But Rick intended to remain firm on this point. "Take it or leave it, Rae."

Frustrated, Rae blew out an angry breath. "I'll take it," she answered.

Sully glanced at her. "I'm not pleased about this, either."

Rae merely glared at him. Her eyebrows narrowed. "I don't believe you."

"Whatever you say," Sully answered.

But one look at his face testified that he obviously *was* pleased.

"Okay, now that that's settled," Rick said, looking relieved, "let me call my men together. Once I explain all this to them, we can get started. Anybody have any objections?" Rick asked, looking from Sully to Rae.

"Wouldn't make any difference if I had them," Rae answered.

Sully laughed. "You sound just like one of my sisters," he told her.

"Give her my condolences the next time you see her," Rae said flippantly as she followed Rick out into the main area.

Sully was right behind her.

Summarizing the events that had transpired, Rick quickly filled in his three deputies, Joe, Gabe and Daniel, about what they needed to do.

Usually able to take most of Rick's notifications in stride without comment, for once, none of the men appeared stoic when they were told about Warren's actual identity and the crime that he had possibly committed.

"So we're not even sure if this dead ranch hand stole the money?" Dan questioned.

Rather than answer the deputy, Rick looked toward Sully. "It's your story," he said. "You want to do the honors?"

"Wynters was the likeliest suspect," Sully answered. "All the information the police have seemed to point to him at least being a person of interest. But the police in Arizona were still working on finding definitive evidence that Wynters actually embezzled the money."

Rae took advantage of the long pause that followed to interject her own thoughts on the matter.

"Well, until they do," she said to the men in the room, "I think we shouldn't mention anything about the possibility that there might be stolen money hidden somewhere around Forever." She looked at each of their faces before continuing. "Something like that can only bring out the worst in people."

"She's right," Rick agreed after a beat. "The last thing any of us want is to have a town full of people running around, trying to beat out everyone else and be the first one who's able to locate the missing money—if the money is even here in Forever," he qualified.

"You might not be giving the town enough credit," Gabe pointed out.

The sheriff had already considered that and come to a conclusion.

"I'd rather not give them enough credit and be proven wrong than watch upstanding citizens turn their backs on everything they've spent years building up just to get a chance of being the one to discover where the money's hidden or buried," Rick told his men.

"*If* it's even here," Rae said. When the men looked at her, she reminded them of what else the man could have done with the money, "Maybe he left the money in some safety-deposit box or even deposited in another bank out of the area," she suggested.

But Sully shook his head. He didn't see that as a possibility.

"You can't deposit that much money in a bank without raising all sorts of red flags with the government. Any amount $10,000 or over draws instant attention."

"Maybe the guy deposits in a lot of different banks," Joe suggested.

"That would make it too many banks to keep track of, not to mention that it would physically require a lot of time to make deposits of $9,999 until the entire sum had been put away," Rick pointed out. "Besides, I only interacted with him a couple of times, but Wynters didn't strike me as being some sort of a master criminal."

"He had to have something on the ball if he ultimately managed to pull off this embezzlement," Rae maintained.

"That might be true, but my gut tells me that he'd want to keep that money somewhere close by. That way, he could get his hands on it at a moment's notice and just take off if he needed to without having to go through all sorts of trouble to get his money," Sully said.

"So, we're agreed?" Rick asked, looking around the room at his deputies as well as at Sully and Rae. "We keep the details of this case a secret for the time being. We can just say that Warren met with some kind of an accident and that we're looking to talk to people who might have seen him that last day so we can piece together exactly what happened to him."

Every one of the four other men in the room either nodded or gave their verbal assent that they were willing to go along with the sheriff's version of the events.

Only Rae remained silent, waiting until the others had all given their opinion.

As their voices faded, she finally spoke up and said, "I think we should tell Miss Joan about this."

Chapter 16

Rae's suggestion initially met with opposition from two of the three deputies. But in the end, everyone was in agreement that telling Miss Joan the whole truth about the man she had taken pity on and sent to work on the J-H Ranch was the only real option they had.

Since she was the one who had brought the matter up, Rae assumed that she should also be the one who was going to tell Miss Joan this part of what was turning out to be an outlandish story.

Sully said nothing until after their assignments had been given out and he and Rae were almost at the diner. And then he spoke up to say, "I'll tell her."

Caught off guard, Rae looked at him. She guessed

why he was volunteering. "I don't need to be protected."

"Nobody's saying anything about protecting you," Sully told her. "You've got nothing to do with this. You didn't get Wynters to embezzle the money, you didn't make him run and come here, posing as a ranch hand, and you're certainly not responsible for killing him." He could see the impatience in her eyes. She was getting ready to argue with him. "Get over yourself, Mulcahy. You are *not* responsible for any of this. And I'm the one who dug up this secret life of his."

A hot answer burned on her tongue. But at the last minute, she stopped herself from saying it. Instead, she rethought the situation.

"I know what you're doing," she told Sully. In her opinion, he was trying to get her to stop feeling guilty about the man's murder. Easier said than done, she thought.

"Good," he declared. "That makes one of us." Because he was just playing this by ear, he thought.

Sully started going up the stairs to the diner. He didn't have to turn around to know that she was right behind him.

"I'm coming with you," she told him in case he had any ideas to the contrary.

He surprised her. He made no attempt to stop her or get her to change her mind and wait for him outside the diner.

"It's a free country," he replied. Pulling open the door, he walked in ahead of her.

"Well, you two are certainly getting to be regular customers," Miss Joan commented before they had even crossed halfway to the counter. Taking a closer look at their faces, Miss Joan glanced over to Marisol, one of the two waitresses on duty that shift. "Take over for me, Marisol," she said.

Not waiting for the young woman to acknowledge the order, Miss Joan made her way around the counter.

"Last booth," she told the duo coming toward her. She pointed a bony finger in that direction for emphasis. Under her watchful eye, they turned around and headed toward the booth.

Bringing up the rear, Miss Joan waited until Sully and Rae sat down before she took her own seat. It wasn't clear if she chose the seat so she could sit next to Rae or if she chose it to face Sully.

"All right, what did you find out?" she asked them. Seeing a look of surprise cross Sully's face, she said, "You obviously came here to tell me something or you wouldn't look as if this was the dress rehearsal for the funeral."

Sully grinned as he marveled at the woman's inherent intuition. "No wonder Uncle Seamus liked you," he commented with a laugh.

Miss Joan merely gave him a look from beneath her hooded eyes. "That was not the only reason," she informed him. "Now talk."

Sully took the lead. As succinctly as possible, he told the woman about everything that Valri had forwarded to him. When he finished, he expected

Miss Joan to express her surprise or display a sense of betrayal, if not both. After all, she had provided Warren/Wynters with a roof over his head and a job while, all along, he'd been a thief looking for a place to hide out.

However, the woman's expression remained completely unchanged.

When she finally spoke, Miss Joan said, "I had a feeling that he wasn't a ranch hand, but I could tell that man definitely needed help, not to mention a place to stay. So I decided the ranch would take a chance on him." Having said that, the woman seemed to transform right in front of them—her period of mourning, if that was what it could be called, was over.

Miss Joan got down to business. "So where are you with the investigation?" she asked.

"Other than finding out Warren's true identity and why he had come so far away from his comfort zone, nowhere," Sully informed her. "We're planning on talking to everyone who was at your party, see if anyone noticed Wynters leaving and if they did, did they happen to see if there was anyone with him."

Miss Joan nodded, giving her blessings to the investigation.

"I'm sorry to say that I didn't see him leaving," she told her ranch foreman. "I did see him talking to Jackson and Garrett, those two brothers who run the Healing Ranch," she explained for Sully's benefit. "I think that was around eight, or a little earlier. I don't recall seeing him after that. But then," she added, "I wasn't exactly looking for him, either. My attention was on Cash and Alma."

"This is good," Sully told the older woman. "This helps us build a time line. You've been a great help, Miss Joan."

Miss Joan had never had any use for flattery. She saw it as an entire waste of breath.

"No, I haven't," she contradicted Sully, dismissing his words. "Let me know if those two boys say anything useful when you question them. And you—" she turned her sharp eyes on Rae "—don't forget to have his back when he carries on his investigation."

Rae flushed. "I really should be getting back to the ranch." After all, that was what Miss Joan had hired her to do. "I haven't been there since we found Warren—I mean, Wynters."

"Don't worry about the ranch," Miss Joan told her. "It's fine. Clint Washburn wound up sending his brother Roy to take care of things until you get back—maybe even for longer than that," she added. "And he's worth more than any three ranch hands put together. I want the two of you focused on finding out who killed that man, whatever he called himself. I don't want to have a killer lurking around in my town," she said with feeling.

"I guess that means you're stuck with me," Rae told Sully as they left the diner. She wouldn't dream of ignoring Miss Joan's instruction.

Sully's smile was easy—and somehow unsettling at the same time, Rae thought.

"I wouldn't exactly call it being stuck," he told her. "Those two brothers Miss Joan said were talking to Wynters, where can I find them?"

"They run the Healing Ranch," she told him. "It's located not too far outside of town."

"The Healing Ranch," Sully repeated. "That sounds more like some kind of a spa. I thought she said that it's a ranch for wayward boys."

"It is," Rae assured him as they walked over to her truck. "That's what's being healed—the boys' antisocial behavior. Jackson and Garrett use horses to help teach the boys who are sent to their ranch a sense of responsibility."

"Horses, eh?" He rolled the idea over in his mind as he got into the truck and buckled up. "I guess that sounds like a pretty good idea." His smile widened as he thought about the possibilities of a ranch like that. "Maybe I'll run that past my uncles at the next family gathering I go to."

She'd started up the truck and pulled out. Sully was already making plans for when he left, she thought. The pang she experienced caught her off guard, surprising her. She felt as if there was a sinking pit where her stomach used to be.

"And when will that be?" she asked, trying to sound as if she was indifferent to the idea, one way or another.

She heard him laugh beside her. "Trying to get rid of me, Mulcahy?"

"No, just wondering how soon I'm going to have to look for another ranch hand, that's all. You might not have noticed," she said with a touch of sarcasm, "but I'm short one ranch hand already. Two if you consider how lazy Rawlings usually is."

"Yeah, I noticed something like that," Sully answered. "For the record, I plan to stick around until this murder gets solved. Maybe longer if you can't find any extra cowboys to hire."

She didn't believe him, at least not about the last part. But for now, she pretended that she did. "I'll hold you to that," she told him.

The smile he gave her told her that he didn't think of that as a threat. It wasn't exactly anything to take to the bank, she thought, but for now she decided that maybe this meant that he really intended to hang around a little longer.

Both of the White Eagle brothers seemed to have their hands full when Rae and Sully arrived at the Healing Ranch. Their tremendous success turning around delinquent boys on the verge of being sent to prison, making them useful members of society, had put the brothers and their ranch on the map.

Since the ranch had come into being, the brothers had had to more than double up their efforts, and even that didn't seem like enough lately. The brothers were looking into expanding the ranch, but only if they could get like-minded people to run it.

Sully managed to corner Jackson first. Jackson was the older of the two and the one who had initially started the school in honor of his late uncle, who had kept him from throwing away his life by going down the wrong path. His uncle had used his ranch to help get the lesson across to the young, hostile Jackson.

The rest, he liked to say, was history.

When Sully questioned him, Jackson recalled the events at the party very clearly.

"Yes, we only talked for a few minutes. To be honest, I didn't know him very well, just that he was working on Miss Joan's ranch. He seemed nice enough, though," Jackson added. "When we finished exchanging pleasantries, he drifted over to toward the Rodriguez brothers." He thought for a moment. "That's the last I remember seeing him." Jackson looked around and spotted his younger brother with one of their latest charges in the corral. "Hey, Garrett," he called over to him.

Garrett finished giving instructions to the boy he was working with, then came over to where Jackson as well as Rae and Sully were standing.

"Did anything strike you as being strange about Warren at Miss Joan's party?" Jackson asked his brother. When the latter looked at him, somewhat confused, Jackson explained, "You know, one of the two wranglers working on the J-H Ranch. He went missing some time before the party at Murphy's was over."

"Strange?" Garrett repeated, thinking. "I don't think so. He did look a little nervous just before he went off to talk to the Rodriguez brothers."

"Nervous?" Rae asked, instantly alert. "Nervous how? Did someone say something to make him nervous?"

But Garret looked at a loss. "I really can't say. If I was to make a guess, it looked as if Cash made him act fidgety, nervous."

"Money made him nervous?" Sully questioned, trying to make sense out of what Garrett was telling them.

"What? No, Cash. Cash Taylor," Garrett emphasized. "At least Warren *looked* as if he was looking in Cash's direction when he suddenly turned as white as a sheet. That was when I saw him making his way over toward the Rodriguez brothers really fast."

"Are you talking about the deputy?" Sully asked. "Gabe Rodriguez?"

Garrett shook his head, "No, no, Gabe's brothers. I didn't see Gabe around until later." One of the boys he'd been working with in the corral called over to Garrett. "Look, do you mind if I go now? I can answer more questions for you later if you want to go on. But I really need to get back to Allen right now," he said, glancing over toward the teen in the corral.

"Sure, go," Sully urged. "That's it for now. Thanks a lot for your help," he added.

Garrett was already on his way back to the corral, walking backward so he still faced the two people who had come to the ranch asking questions.

"Sure. Anything Jackson and I can do to help with this investigation, just say the word. I don't like the fact that someone murdered someone in Forever, even if that person wasn't one of our own."

* * *

As it turned out, Cash was out of town on business, so Sully and Rae weren't able to ask him any questions about why Wynters might have looked nervous when he saw the lawyer—or if Garrett had misread the scene.

Since Cash wouldn't be back until the next day, Sully and Rae went on questioning some of the other citizens who had been at Murphy's. Each so-called lead trickled into the next person they interviewed. However, after doing this for the remainder of the day, no tangible information was actually gleaned pointing to anyone.

"I think my brain hurts," Rae said to Sully late that evening when they both collapsed onto the worn leather sofa in the living room.

They had been at it all day and finally came back to the ranch long after dark.

Despite having Clint Washburn's brother Roy— and another ranch hand—pitching in at the ranch and taking care of the horses, Rae felt it was her responsibility to make sure that all was well. This meant going to see things at the stable for herself.

The stalls were all cleaned out with fresh hay spread out in place of the old, and all the horses had fresh feed waiting for them.

Although she was satisfied that the job had been well done, for the first time since she'd been fifteen, Rae felt as if she wasn't needed.

Sully had stretched out his long, lanky frame next

to hers in the living room, looking like someone who had no intentions of moving any more than absolutely necessary any time soon.

"You'll get used to it," he told her.

She assumed he was referring to her comment about the state of her brain.

"I don't know about that," she answered. "Aches and pains I can handle. I once broke my wrist and still managed to get through the day before Miss Joan caught on and forced me to go see the doctor. But this is different. I feel really, *really* drained and tried. The kind of tired that if the sofa was on fire, I still wouldn't be able to get up."

Sully laughed at the image she'd just painted. "Oh, you'd be surprised at how fast you could move if there was a fire underneath you. And, personally, you turned out to be a lot stronger than I thought you were." He paused a moment, looking at her, his head being the only thing he was able to move. "In fact, I'm going to give you the ultimate compliment. You are actually strong enough to be an honorary Cavanaugh."

Taking a deep breath, Rae turned her head to look at him, although it took effort.

"I'm flattered," she told him, allowing a laugh to escape her lips.

"You should be. Not everyone can measure up to that or be that strong. As a matter of fact, it takes a steel resolve and a large amount of stubbornness. A hell of a lot of stubbornness," he emphasized.

And as he said it, he felt something stirring within him.

A moment ago, Sully would have sworn he was drained. As drained, both physically and mentally, as Rae had just said she was. But after having turned to look at her, he found that he had mysteriously gotten a second wind from somewhere, one that if not totally rejuvenating him at least gave him the energy to cut the small amount of distance that had been between them down to much less than half that.

And even less than that.

Without fully knowing how, he had managed to shift so that he was less than a hairbreadth away from her.

Sully told himself that he should move. That right now he was far too close to her and that would only lead to him making a mistake. Besides, he'd already kissed Rae. Twice. It wasn't as if he was motivated by a sense of adventure or exploration.

But that was just it. He *had* kissed her before, and what was motivating him now wasn't curiosity—it was a desire to repeat the sensation, to feel what he already knew he would feel, except perhaps more so.

This was absurd.

He was in the middle of an investigation, for Pete's sake. He didn't have time to behave like some impressionable adolescent.

And yet…

And yet everything inside his body suddenly wanted to experience that rejuvenating kiss one more time. To feel as if the weight of the world wasn't threatening to come down on his shoulders, pressing him to the ground. All he wanted to was to feel the way he had when he had been a teenager, a time when nothing else mattered and the evening was endless with possibilities.

You're going to regret this, a little voice in his head warned him.

But Sully had never listened to the voice in his head, he only listened to his gut—and his gut was telling him to kiss Rae.

Chapter 17

Every single pulse point in her body was pounding wildly in ever-growing anticipation. She was suddenly a symphony of needs and desires, and it had all taken her totally and utterly by surprise.

Only a second ago, Rae could have sworn that after the full day they had just put in, she was utterly spent.

Yet the single unspoken promise of what was to come telegraphed itself through her body, causing every nerve ending she had to stand at attention—waiting.

Hoping.

The air in her lungs had stopped moving, almost solidifying.

She was literally holding her breath.

Was he going to kiss her? Or would he draw away at the last moment because he didn't want to mix business with pleasure, as if he felt that would somehow wind up degrading both?

The moment stretched out, feeling as if it was lasting a lifetime.

The ache inside her grew.

"Are you going to make me kiss you?" she asked. Her voice seemed to echo in her head.

Rather than move in, or pull back, Sully asked her, "Do you want to?"

She could have screamed. "What I don't want, Cavanaugh, is to verbally fill out some questionnaire about—"

Rae didn't get a chance to finish. She didn't have to. Sully had his answer.

His lips found hers, and with almost aching precision, the moment was suddenly ignited, setting off flames all around her that were ten feet tall.

What began almost in slow motion suddenly seemed to explode. Needs took over, demanding satisfaction. Demanding tribute.

Suddenly, that fire they had just discussed in hypothetical terms became very, very real. It raced through her limbs, feeding on everything in its path, obliterating it.

She didn't know it, but she was experiencing a complete mirror image of what was happening to him right at the same time.

The rest of what was happening became almost a blur, a heated, glorious blur of clothing disappearing. Of incredibly hot, life-affirming, demanding kisses, of body parts threatening to melt into throbbing heaps as possessing hands and questing lips seemed to touch just about everywhere, leaving no part unconquered.

Flames were being fanned rather than being set to rest.

Rae had never imagined, not even in her wildest dreams, that making love with someone could ever feel like this. Her very thoughts were incinerated, vanishing from existence to be replaced by the urgent supplication beating in her brain: more.

She wanted more.

The more he touched her, kissed her, caused her body to spontaneously writhe and twist almost as if it was a separate entity, the more she *wanted* him to touch her, to kiss her.

To caress her.

Struggling to catch her breath, Rae did her best to turn the tables on him. She wanted nothing more than to return the favor by making Sully's body sing the way he was making hers.

Stunned, Sully didn't know what to think at first. Because she had surprised him. In each relationship he'd had, in each encounter, he had always been the one to do the pleasuring. That was how he had gotten his own pleasure.

To suddenly be on the receiving end of the sensations he had always bestowed was something entirely new for him. Suddenly, the pleasure threshold that existed had been surmounted—and surpassed.

Engaged in a passionate, exquisite contest of one-upmanship, they wound up tumbling from the sofa without even realizing it at first.

Their bodies remained tangled together as they took turns delivering and receiving volleys of almost surreal pleasure to one another.

Her head was spinning, but she was still aware of every movement his body made along hers. He'd done wondrous things with his mouth and tongue, causing one climax after another to burst through her, consuming every square inch of her until she was certain that she was totally spent—only to realize that she craved more.

And then, as the entire world was swirling, seeming to spin almost out of control all around her, Rae caught her breath as she felt Sully enter her.

Not as if he was storming the gates, but slowly, gently.

Teasingly.

Which only created yet another vast, endless ache within her.

Rae raised her hips, urging him to move faster. To bring that final, deliciously beautiful explosion vibrating all through her.

She mimicked his movements; he increased the tempo until neither knew who was in the lead and who was following.

They both were.

One final thrust did it, brought them both up to the highest peak.

Simultaneously.

Fireworks and stardust seemed to rain down all around them, and they both held on to that one moment for as long as they could—aching for it to go on just a little longer.

The beat of their hearts mimicking one another was all they were aware of.

Slowly, the beat muted, slipping away.

Sully didn't want to let her go, didn't want to allow this moment to slip into the past. If he could, he would have gone on holding Rae forever.

He knew that he couldn't.

Still, he kept one arm tucked around her, holding Rae to him as if she was something very precious, and the second he let go, she would disappear. Along with the moment.

"So I guess you *can* move if there's a fire under you," he teased.

She turned her head toward him. "Meaning you?" she asked. "Are you the fire?"

He felt her hair as it brushed against his cheek. Why did that feel so sensual? And why in heaven's name, after making love with her like some possessed wild man, did he feel himself wanting her again with a verve that left him speechless?

"I'll be anything you want me to be," he whispered almost hoarsely.

She'd been with three men in her entire life. Each of them had managed to fill the moment while it was happening. But none had ever managed to fill her soul.

Yet this man who was almost already gone out of

her life, he had filled the terrible emptiness that she assumed was her heart.

She was being self-destructive. There was no doubt about it in her mind. Why else would she have allowed herself to respond like this, to have actual *feelings* for someone who she knew for a fact was only temporarily in her life?

Who would be leaving all too soon, disappearing from her life forever? Leaving an insurmountable ache in his place?

She felt tears dampening her lashes and bit the inside of her bottom lip, willing the tears to go away. Tomorrow would be here fast enough, taking him away from her. If not tomorrow, then the day after tomorrow. But she still had now.

And now was all she wanted.

"Good," she whispered, lacing her arms around his neck, surrendering herself to him. "Because I need that fire."

Sully came very close to groaning, feeling his body responding to her all over again.

"One fire coming up," he told her, his voice growing thick just before his mouth covered hers.

The fire went on for a long time.

Morning found them in her bed. She'd taken him there with her and they had made love one final time before exhaustion finally claimed them both.

They'd slept straight through until morning, when beams of sunlight shining into the room had nudged them awake.

Not wanting Sully to feel as if he owed her any morning-after conversation, Rae quickly grabbed her clothes and hurried into the bathroom, where she dressed in record time.

"Cash should be back sometime within the next couple of hours," she told him, doing her best to sound like she was all business and not as if just being close to him like this made her want him all over again. "We should get to his office if we want to question him. We can ask him about any conversation he might have had with Wynters before his clients start coming in. He might not have any time—or want to—talk at that point."

Sully shoved his hands into his pockets. It was either that or he'd wind up reaching for her.

"If we want to get to him first thing, we should go to his house, not the office. I'm sure that when he got home from his business trip, Cash went straight home to his wife," Sully pointed out.

She was usually sharper than that, she upbraided herself.

"You're right," Rae agreed. "Want breakfast?" she asked, realizing that they hadn't had any dinner last night. Lovemaking had usurped hunger.

But hunger was back.

For a moment, Sully considered her suggestion. If they stayed here for breakfast, he knew what was bound to happen. With no one around to interrupt them, one thing would easily lead to another, especially since he wanted her.

He needed to focus on solving this crime. A lot

of people were waiting for answers, and no one was going to sleep easy in their beds until whoever had committed this murder was caught.

He had to keep the bigger picture in mind—even though all he could think of was Rae.

"Why don't we get some breakfast at the diner before we go talk to Cash?" he suggested.

Rae read between the lines. She knew what Sully was doing.

She smiled at him. "Safety in numbers, is that it, Detective?"

Sully saw no reason to pretend he didn't know what she was talking about. He respected her thought process too much.

"Something like that," he acknowledged.

Her smiled widened. It was nice to know that this had affected both of them.

"Okay. I'll just talk to Clint's brother to let him know where we'll be this morning and then we can get going," she told him.

Just as she opened the door, he put his hand on her arm. She turned to look at him quizzically. "What?"

"You do know that you can stay here and see to the ranch if you're worried about how things are going," Sully reminded her.

"Actually, for the first time in a long time, I am *not* worried about how things are going on the ranch. Turns out that Washburn's really good at running a ranch. From what I gather, he even got Rawlings to put in a full day's work with the horses."

"You're good at getting Rawlings to pull his weight, too," Sully pointed out loyally.

"No, I got Rawlings to put in what *looked* like a full day's work. On closer examination, I found that he kept cutting corners, and he made himself scarce whenever possible. Washburn, on the other hand, has him reporting in at regular intervals. Things are getting done," she said with satisfaction.

"Does that bother you?" Sully asked her out of the blue as they were leaving the house.

She wasn't sure what he was asking about. Rae got in behind the steering wheel. "Does *what* bother me?"

He got in on the passenger side. "The fact that Washburn has everything under control and running so well according to what you just said."

"That would be petty," she said, the truck humming to life as she turned the key. "This is Miss Joan's ranch. She gave me a break by giving me a job here. It's just that I'd hate to see it go under because she did a good deed for someone else in need." She drove toward the road leading from the ranch into town. "We both know that as a ranch hand, Rawlings is a regular sloth. If Washburn can get some work out of him, more power to him. I'm all for it."

Sully smiled as they continued on into town. "That's very fair of you," he told her.

"Well, Miss Joan's always been very fair to me," she said. "I can't allow my ego to get in the way of repaying her."

"You don't have an ego," Sully observed.

She was touched, but not taken in. Rae spared him a quick glance.

"Despite what happened last night between us, you don't know anything about me, Cavanaugh," she informed him.

"Oh, I don't know," Sully answered loftily. "I'm a pretty good judge of character."

"Sure you are," she said, her voice dripping with sarcasm.

He nodded. "You're selfless, a hard worker and very passionate about things you care about."

"I sound terrific," she quipped.

He took no notice of her sarcasm. "That's because you are," he told her.

She slanted a glance at Sully, then decided that it just might be simpler and safer all around if music filled the inside of the truck's cab rather than the sound of their voices. At least then she wouldn't feel so embarrassed and at a loss for words.

"Any progress?" Miss Joan asked when she saw them approaching the counter.

Several people were having their breakfast at the counter. They turned to see who had walked in, prompted by idle curiosity and/or a desire to know who Miss Joan was talking to and what the answer to her question was going to be. It was the locals' version of reality TV, Forever-style.

Sully slid onto a stool and leaned in, his body language telling the older woman that what he was about to share with her was for her ears alone.

Miss Joan immediately understood. "Rear table," she said.

Sully and Rae followed Miss Joan, just as they had the first time she'd indicated where she wanted them to sit in order to have privacy.

This time Miss Joan took her seat first, waiting for them to sit and speak.

"We talked to a number of people yesterday, and it hasn't led us anywhere yet," Sully told her. "Although Garrett did mention that he thought Wynters looked spooked when he saw Cash."

"Cash?" Miss Joan repeated. "You mean my grandson?" It was obvious that the information was not what she'd expected. "Why on earth would Wynters be scared by my grandson?"

"We were hoping to talk to Cash and find out," Sully explained. "Turns that your grandson was out of town yesterday."

"I know," Miss Joan responded.

Sully was beginning to believe that what everyone said was true—there was nothing that went on in Forever that the woman wasn't aware of. He decided to ask her first.

"Any idea why Wynters would be afraid of your grandson?" he pressed.

Miss Joan thought a moment. "He consults on out-of-state cases sometimes. Maybe Wynters thought he recognized him, or maybe he crossed paths with Cash while he was still in his other identity. I guess you're going to have to talk to Cash to find out. It could just be that Wynters wasn't looking at Cash but someone else near Cash," the woman speculated.

"I believe that this is where that phrase comes into play," he said after they had eaten and were leaving the diner.

"What phrase?" Rae asked.

"'So near and yet so far,'" Sully answered matter-of-factly.

Chapter 18

Rae pulled up her truck in front of Cash's house just as he was about to leave for the law office he shared with Olivia Blayne-Santiago, the sheriff's wife.

Cash stopped as he was about to close the door behind him. Surprised to see the detective from California and Rae on his doorstep, he commented, "This must be really urgent if you came to my house instead of the office."

"We would have made an appointment for yesterday, but your partner told us that you were out of town for the day," Sully told the lawyer.

"Well, I'm here now." Shifting his briefcase to his other hand, Cash pushed open his front door and gestured for Sully and Rae to follow him inside. "Alma's still asleep," he explained. "This pregnancy is really wiping her out."

"We won't wake her up," Rae promised as she and Sully entered behind Cash.

He led them to the table in the dining room and took a seat. "What can I do for you?" he asked as they followed suit.

"We're asking everyone who was at Murphy's for your party if they could remember seeing what time John Warren left," Rae told Cash.

Since they didn't know if Miss Joan had said anything to her grandson about what had happened or if he even knew that Warren was an alias, she decided it might be simpler to just refer to the dead man by the name he'd used when he'd first arrived.

"John Warren," Cash repeated. They could see by his expression that he was drawing a blank. And then suddenly the light seemed to dawn. "You're talking about that man who Miss Joan had working on the ranch she and my grandfather own, right?" Cash asked, looking from Sully to Rae. "The one who was found dead?"

"Right," Sully responded. Well, it seemed that Cash knew that much, he thought, but then, the gossip mill had been happily at work, so it stood to reason he would know about the man being found dead. He still proceeded with caution. "When we questioned one of the brothers running the Healing Ranch, he mentioned that he thought Warren looked a little nervous when he saw you there." Sully watched the lawyer's face closely, looking for any sort of a reaction. "Would he have had any reason to be?"

Cash looked genuinely baffled. "I didn't know the man," he told them. "To be honest, I wouldn't have been able to pick him out of a crowd. I'm not involved in that part of my grandfather and Miss Joan's business. I just handle their legal papers."

"If you don't mind my saying so, there can't be much money to be made registering deeds and filing wills in a small town like Forever," Sully commented.

It was obvious that he was asking Cash how he managed to make a living doing that.

"You're right," Cash answered. "That's why I also do consulting work for a few out-of-state firms, as well." Then, before the detective could ask him, Cash summarized what he did for those firms. "I set up their 401(k)s, make sure all the legal filings are done correctly, things of that nature. Mostly deal with the red tape they don't want to bother with."

"Do you do that for a lot of firms?" Rae asked.

"I'd say there's a dozen or so right now. I've got all the firms listed at the office." He looked at the duo, his curiosity aroused. "Why? How does this tie in with our dead man?"

"We're just fishing," Sully admitted. "For all we know, it wasn't even you that Warren was looking at."

Since he didn't know the man, that made sense to Cash. "You're probably right, but if there's anything

I can do to help you push this investigation along, all you have to do is tell me."

Rae looked at Sully, waiting for him to ask the logical question. When he didn't, she did it herself. "Would you mind giving us that list you mentioned, the one with the names of all the companies you consult for?" Rae asked.

"Sure," he responded. "It's public knowledge, so I wouldn't be giving away any secrets. I'll get to it first thing," he promised, rising. "Now if you don't have any more questions, I've got a lot of catching up to do at the office. The owners of one of the companies I service are all redoing their wills and want to get them signed, recorded and filed as soon as possible. I'll be flying out again tomorrow," he interjected in case they needed to talk to him then.

Cash had caught his attention. Sully wouldn't have been able to say exactly what suddenly made an alarm go off in his head. He supposed he could just point to the old standby, that his Cavanaugh gut had alerted him.

Whatever the reason, he looked at Cash and asked, "What's the name of that company?"

"Hathaway, Montgomery and Finch." It was a twenty-three-year-old company with an excellent reputation—until recently. "Why do you ask?"

"Let me guess," Sully said, easing into the scenario. "The owners are restructuring everything that has to do with their business because half a million dollars was embezzled from their funds. They don't want it to be public knowledge yet because they're looking to contain the situation. But they're not all that hopeful about it."

Cash's jaw dropped open. "How did you—?" Stunned speechless for a second, Cash couldn't complete his sentence.

Sully exchanged looks with Rae and made a judgment call. No one else beside the sheriff and his deputies—and Miss Joan—knew the details surrounding Wynters's case. He decided that it was time to let one more person into the exclusive club.

"John Warren was actually Jefferson Wynters," he told Cash. "He was working on your grandparents' ranch, pretending to be a wrangler, because he was hiding out."

"Hiding?" Cash echoed, still very lost. None of this was making any sense to him. "Hiding from who?"

That question was easy to answer. It was all the other questions that baffled them. "The people he had embezzled half a million dollars from."

"Half a million dollars?" Cash echoed. He was having trouble absorbing the information. "You're not saying what I think you're saying, are you?"

"That Jefferson Wynters was an accountant at Hathaway, Montgomery and Finch, the company that ran an assisted-living facility in Prescott, Arizona. And that it's believed that he somehow embezzled half a million dollars from the company and took off."

Cash was still having trouble wrapping his mind around the information that the detective was telling him. "If Warren was actually this accountant named Wynters who stole all that money, where's the money right now?"

"A very good question," Rae answered. "From the looks of it, someone killed him for it."

"Or killed him trying to find out where he hid it," Sully said, raising the other viable possibility.

"Which brings us back to trying to find out when Wynters left and if he was alone when he did," Rae told the lawyer.

"Even if he did leave with someone, that someone might not have been the one to kill him," Cash said, trying to look at the situation from all angles.

"You're right," Sully agreed. "But that person might have seen someone following Wynters and *that* person was the one who ultimately killed him. We'll follow you to the office and get that list just in case there's something we're overlooking," he told Cash.

The other man nodded. "Anything I can do to help out," he said.

They all filed out to his driveway. Cash got into his car. Rae and Sully followed in her truck.

It felt as if they were going around and around with all these theories, but Sully wanted to lay everything out—and then start eliminating them one by one.

"What we have here is a whole bunch of conjecture," Rae lamented as she drove to the law office.

"Maybe," Sully agreed, "but it seems clear that Wynters must have recognized Cash and that spooked him enough to get him to leave." The theory was evolving as he talked it out. "Maybe he even decided that it wasn't safe in Forever anymore."

Rae nodded. "So he packed up and left," she agreed. "One question, though."

"Go ahead," Sully said.

"Why would Wynters even come to Forever?" It seemed like too much of a coincidence to her. "It's not as if everyone knows about it. Other than the Healing Ranch, it's not known for anything."

"That's just the point," Sully told her. "The lawyer the firm has coming out to do their legal papers comes from Forever. One of the owners probably talked about Forever being a postage stamp–size town where nothing ever happens and Wynters overhears them saying that.

"The name sticks in the back of his head, and when he finally decides it's time to make off with the money he embezzled, he assumes that no one would ever think to look for him in a place like Forever. He probably didn't realize that the company's lawyer actually *lives* here. Not until he sees Cash and puts two and two together," Sully concluded.

"So you're thinking that was what made him take off with the money," Rae guessed.

"That's the only thing that makes sense," Sully replied.

She tended to agree. "Then where *is* the money?"

"With whoever killed and buried him." That, too, was the only thing that made sense, Sully thought. And then something hit him. "We went about this all wrong. We shouldn't be talking to everyone who attended the party at Murphy's. We should be talking to the people in the area who *didn't* attend."

Rae's eyes widened. "Because the people at the party are each other's alibis," she concluded.

"Exactly."

They went back to Miss Joan.

"Well, you two didn't swallow a canary yet, but you look like you're definitely closing in on one," the older woman said when she saw them walking into the diner. Hazel eyes quickly assessed the duo. "What do you need from me?"

Sully laughed softly. "You have definitely made second-guessing into an art form," he marveled.

Miss Joan's eyes rose to his. "I never guess," she informed him in her no-nonsense voice.

"My mistake," Sully said, managing to keep a smile from his lips.

Miss Joan nodded, but just barely. "You're entitled, boy," she told him magnanimously. "Now what is it you need from me?"

"The guest list from the party you threw for Cash and Alma," Sully told her.

That way, he could focus on the people who weren't on the list.

"There was no list," Miss Joan told him. "It was an open invitation to everyone."

The information surprised Sully. The similarities between Miss Joan and his uncle Andrew astonished him. Miss Joan had a sharp tongue while his uncle was soft-spoken, but both were highly respected by the people they dealt with.

"There had to be some people you excluded," Sully insisted.

"I didn't do the excluding," Miss Joan told him. "Those who didn't attend excluded themselves. It was completely their choice, not mine."

Sully sighed. "We're back to having to interview everyone."

"Not everyone," Miss Joan corrected. "Just the ones you haven't interviewed yet."

Sully inclined his head. The woman was right—as always. He struggled not to allow his frustration to get the better of him.

"We need to tell the sheriff and his deputies about what you found," Rae told Sully as they walked out of the diner.

He realized that with everything that they had been rethinking, he had almost forgotten about sharing all this with the police.

"You mean what *we* found," Sully corrected.

Rae was surprised at the way he'd put it. "You mean that you're not going to be territorial about this?"

He laughed. That was not the way he'd been raised. He'd cut his teeth on team effort, not on being a glory hound.

"When this is all behind us, Mulcahy, I have *got* to take you with me to Aurora to meet my family. There is no such thing as being territorial when you're a

Cavanaugh. It's all a joint effort no matter what the puzzle turns out to be."

She thought of how he had come up with the information they were using. "You mean like when you called your cousin Valri and your cousin's wife, that medical examiner." The woman's name escaped her at the moment.

Sully smiled at her as they cut across the street to get to the sheriff's office. "You're catching on," he told her.

He sounded pleased, she thought. Why, she had no idea. The man was definitely an enigma.

Neither the sheriff nor any of his deputies were in the office when they walked in. The only person who *was* there was Alvin Hayes.

Alvin was a recent high school graduate who was still attempting to figure out what he wanted to do with his life. In the interim, in order to earn some money, he worked part-time for the sheriff's office, answering the phones. Most of the time, since the phones were usually silent, Alvin fixed coffee, filed reports and occasionally swept up.

At the moment, he was sitting at his desk, staring off into space and whistling some tuneless song.

"Where is everyone?" Sully asked him.

Alvin instantly snapped to attention when he realized who had walked in. He looked uneasy in Sully's presence and mumbled his answer so low, it wasn't even remotely audible.

"Try again," Sully told him patiently.

Alvin cleared his throat. This time, his words were audible, if somewhat shaky.

"They're all out questioning people who were at Miss Joan's party. If you check on Murphy's and Mick's Garage, you might see a couple of them," Alvin said, his Adam's apple bobbing prominently up and down his rather long throat.

Alvin was probably right, but that would involve talking to the deputies and Rick one at a time, Sully thought, and he wanted to see them all together. He didn't feel like having to repeat this newest briefing a total of four times. It would be wasting time.

"Can you call them and ask them to come back to the office?" Sully requested.

On his feet, Alvin looked even more gangly. "You mean all of them?" he asked uncertainly. He was accustomed to getting his orders from the sheriff and looked undecided about just what to do since Sully was giving him the order.

"That would work, yes," Sully answered, cutting the teenager some slack.

"Well, I guess I can do that, but—" Alvin's voice trailed off and his uncertainty seemed to rise in startling proportions.

He had no intentions of debating this with Alvin. "Do it," Sully instructed.

"They won't get mad at you," Rae promised, taking a guess at the reason behind Alvin's reticence to call the sheriff. "You're only following the detective's instructions, and the sheriff would want you to do that."

Still looking somewhat hesitant, Alvin got on the radio, pushed a button and then hit the com line. The last step enabled him to get in touch with all four men who were part of the sheriff's department at once.

It was the first time he'd ever used the radio for that purpose, and he looked rather startled when he heard the com line come to life.

"Um, Sheriff?" Alvin began nervously, his voice all but cracking. "Over," he added belatedly.

"What did I tell you about the radio, Alvin, over?" Rick asked patiently.

"To stay off it." Alvin's voice cracked. He waited until he felt he could confidently utter, "Over."

"That's right. So why are you on it, over?"

Alvin swallowed, slanting a look in Rae's direction, silently asking for backup. "Because Miss Rae said you wouldn't be mad at me. Over."

"Is she there with you, Alvin. Over?" Rick asked.

"Yes, sir, over."

"Put her on, over," Rick told him in a patient voice that sounded as if it was nearing its end.

Alvin turned around only to almost bump into Rae. "He wants me to put you on."

"I heard, Alvin," she assured him. "Sheriff, this is Rae. I think you and the deputies all need to come in. Over."

"You have the killer, over?" There was no missing the hopeful note in his voice.

"No, but we have another piece of the puzzle, over," she informed him.

"A large piece," Sully said, temporarily taking the radio from her to relay the message to Rick. "Over."

"We'll be there in ten, over and out," Rick told them.

Rae handed the radio receiver back to Alvin. The latter took it and looked at her with huge eyes that seemed as if they were about to fall out at any second. "He didn't sound mad, did he?" he asked, seeking reassurance.

"No," Rae answered, trying to calm the nervous teen. "He didn't, Alvin."

She just hoped the sheriff wouldn't be disappointed when he learned about this newest development.

Chapter 19

Rick and his deputies arrived back at the office almost at the same time.

They all pooled their information, with Sully and Rae going first, telling the others that in all likelihood Wynters recognized Cash Taylor as the lawyer who consulted for the firm where he worked. He'd taken off before Cash could recognize him and possibly make the connection between Wynters and the missing money.

"Billy Tanner said he saw Wynters leaving. Nobody was with him," Gabe told them.

"Liam Murphy told me the same thing when I questioned him," Daniel said to the group, adding, "Liam also said he saw Wynters slipping out through the back doors where the saloon's deliveries are made. It was around the time when he and his band finished their second set."

Rae tried to think back to that evening, pinning down a time. "I'd say that would have been around seven, give or take a few minutes."

"Sounds about right," Sully recalled. He looked at the others for confirmation. The sheriff nodded, as did his senior deputy.

"That means that Wynters had to have gotten a ride from somebody that night," Rae said. "He couldn't have just walked back to the ranch. It was much too far from town, especially since Wynters was in a hurry to leave."

"Okay," Rick said, turning toward his deputies, "new question. Who gave Wynters, or as most of the people in town still think of him, Warren a ride back to the ranch—or at least saw someone who gave him a ride?"

"I'd start by checking the people in the houses that either face Murphy's or are on either side of the saloon," Sully told the gathering. "You never know, we might get lucky. Maybe someone who either came back early or didn't go to the party for some reason was looking out their window and saw something." And then he looked at the sheriff and realized that in his desire to make some headway, he might have overstepped some boundaries. "Just a suggestion," he added.

"And a damn good one," Rick told Sully as well as the men under him. "All right, you heard the detective. Fan out and start knocking on doors, people."

"Sheriff—" Sully cornered the man as the deputies went back out again to question more of Forever's residents. "Did you get anything new from the medical examiner when he redid the autopsy?"

"Cause of death was just what we all thought," Rick confirmed. "Wynters received two fatal stab wounds right to the heart."

Sully could see by the sheriff's expression that there was more. "Anything else?" he asked.

"Yes," Rick answered. "The ME also found bruising on Wynters's arms, and there's a wide gash on the back of the man's head."

"The killer knocked him out with a rock first?" Rae questioned, trying to get a clearer picture of the events that came just before the man was murdered.

"Either that, or Wynters fell and hit his head against a rock," Sully speculated.

This puts things in a different light, Rae thought. She put the question to the sheriff. "Could that have been the cause of death?"

"That hasn't been determined yet," the sheriff told them.

Rae was still trying to work things out in her head. "But if that gash on the back of his head does turn out to be the cause of death, then why did the killer stab him, too?" It seemed like overkill to her.

Sully played with the pieces in his mind. "Maybe to cover up the accident—if it was an accident—make it seem like Wynters was killed during a robbery," the detective theorized.

Rae shook her head. That didn't sound right to

her. "I once read somewhere that if you hear hoof-beats, think horses, not zebras."

"Are you saying that you feel I'm overthinking this?" Sully asked her.

Rae decided to restate what they already knew to be true. "Wynters embezzled money and took off. When he recognized Cash, he made another run for it. But the money's missing. The simplest assumption is that someone killed him to get their hands on it."

"It *sounds* plausible," Sully readily agreed, but there was still something nagging at him.

"Maybe we'll get our answers when we find who-ever drove Wynters back to the ranch," Rick said, interrupting the debate.

"Hey, Sheriff, I might have found someone who can help with that," Daniel announced as he walked into the office. The tall deputy wasn't alone. With him was a very tired-looking young woman who looked as if she hadn't slept in days.

"Why don't you take a seat, Edna?" Rick told her, turning a chair around so that all she had to do was drop into it. Which she did. "Did you happen to see anything last Saturday?" he asked, trying to keep his question as vague as possible. He didn't want to lead the woman to an answer—he wanted her to be the one to offer up the information.

"My baby is colicky," Edna began, explaining why she looked as tired as she did. "I've been up every night for a week, walking the floor with him.

Jim's working so he needs his sleep," she explained, referring to her husband and the father of her baby.

She was getting off track, Rae thought. "You're a good wife and mother, Edna," she told the woman soothingly. "You probably feel like you covered a lot of miles walking back and forth with your son, trying to get him to fall asleep."

Edna sighed in agreement. "Miles and miles," the young woman said.

Rae watched the young mother's face. "You probably looked out the window, trying to distract yourself while you were doing all that walking," Rae continued.

Edna nodded. "I had to. A couple of times I felt like I was losing my mind."

"Totally understandable," Rae told the young mother. Looking at the others, she could see that they were all waiting for her to get the woman to tell them what she saw. "Did you see anything interesting when you looked out your window?" Rae asked, gently trying to steer Edna in the right direction.

Edna sighed. "There really wasn't much to see. It felt like everyone in town but me and the baby were at Murphy's that night, having a good time. Even my Jim went," she pouted.

"So you didn't see anything," Sully asked, trying to move her along.

"I didn't say that," Edna protested. "I saw this stranger—" She paused for a minute, trying to state this just the right way. "—I think he's one of Miss Joan's charity cases—anyway, he got in the middle of the street and waved his hands so he could stop someone driving a truck. He said something to the driver, and then he got in and they both drove off."

"Did you see who was driving the truck?" Rick prodded the woman, trying not to sound too excited.

Like the others, he didn't want to influence Edna and have her possibly remember something that *hadn't* happened.

Edna nodded, her light brown hair falling into her face. She pushed her hair behind her ear. "It was one of the McGee twins," she answered. "Couldn't tell you which one, though."

It was obviously all the woman had to offer. Rick helped Edna to her feet, smiling at her.

"You've been a great help, Edna," he told her.

She looked pleased, but she was still very tired as she nodded. "I've got to get back, Sheriff. I left Jim with the baby. He's a good husband, but he doesn't know the first thing about taking care of a crying baby."

"Maybe you could show him what to do," Rick suggested, escorting the woman to the front door. "Men don't like feeling helpless. All they need is a little guidance."

"Where would I find the McGee twins?" Sully asked the minute the door had closed behind Edna.

"On their family's ranch would be my guess," the sheriff said. "They have a spread due east of Forever. It's a cattle ranch. I'll drive," he told Sully as he led the way out the door.

"I'm coming, too," Rae announced, hurrying after the two men.

Rick merely laughed warmly. "Kind of figured you would."

The McGee ranch wasn't too far out of town. Driving fast, it took about forty-five minutes to reach it.

Rick was the first one out of the truck. Striding up to the front door, he knocked on it. The door opened almost immediately.

"I need to talk to your boys, Jacob," Rick told the deeply tanned, sun-wrinkled older man standing on the other side of it.

The senior McGee had just come into the house to wash off some dust from his face and hands a few minutes before the sheriff had pulled up in his truck.

Jacob McGee did not look happy to be on the receiving end of the sheriff's greeting. The scowl on his face went clear down to the bone.

"What've they done now?" Jacob asked wearily.

Jacob's wife, Peggy, pushed the door open all the way. "Why don't you let the man talk before you jump to conclusions, Jake?"

Jacob's scowl deepened even more as he ignored his wife.

"I'll take you to them," he volunteered, grabbing his hat from a hook by the door as he walked out.

"Jake—" his wife called after him, her voice laced with frustration.

Rick paused to reassure the woman. "There's

nothing to worry about, Mrs. McGee," he told her. "I just need to ask your sons a few questions."

"They didn't do anything," Peggy McGee called out after the men.

"That's just the problem. They *never* do anything," McGee grumbled, putting distance between himself and the woman in the doorway.

Rather than give them directions where to find his sons, Jacob McGee insisted on driving them to where both his sons were working, along with a couple of other ranch hands.

Rae couldn't help thinking how much larger this ranch was in size than the one she ran for Miss Joan and her husband. But then, that ranch wasn't being run for a profit, the way this one obviously was.

"The sheriff here wants to talk to you boys," Jacob said to his sons the moment he got out of his truck. "So listen up," he ordered.

Jacob's sons stopped working and exchanged looks. "We haven't done anything, Sheriff," one of the twins said defensively.

At six-three, with wheat-colored hair and green eyes, Bob and Bill were identical twins whose own father couldn't tell them apart from a distance.

Rick kept his voice low and friendly as he told the twins why he was there. "Edna Miller said she saw one of you boys pick up John Warren and give him a ride last Saturday. Where did you take him?" the sheriff asked mildly.

"I gave him a ride to the J-H Ranch," Bob said,

stepping forward. "He flagged me down, so I had to stop."

"And you brought him to the ranch?" Sully asked.

"Sure," Bob confirmed, adding defensively, "it's what he asked me to do. It was on my way home anyway. Why?" he asked, looking from the sheriff to the man with him. His brow furrowed. "Is he claiming something different?"

"Where on the ranch did you drop him?" Rae asked.

Bob looked at her, obviously confused why he was being questioned this way. "He wanted me to bring him to the bunkhouse. He gave me ten bucks to do it," he said, as if that explained everything.

And then he added nervously, "I didn't see any harm in it, since he worked on the ranch and all. Why? Wasn't I supposed to? Did you fire him or something?" he asked Rae, aware that she was the one who ran the ranch for Miss Joan, even though it seemed ludicrous to him.

Although he asked Rae the question, it was Sully who spoke up. "Did you see anyone else around when you dropped Warren off at the bunkhouse?"

"I wasn't looking for anyone else," Bob practically whinnied. He looked from Sully to the sheriff. "What's this all about?" he asked.

"Yeah, what's this all about?" Bill echoed.

"How about Rawlings?" Rae asked Bob suddenly. "Did you see him there?"

Bob shrugged, his shoulders moving beneath his gingham shirt like loose rocks searching for a resting place. "I saw somebody in the background when Warren opened the door to go in, but I dunno who it was. I was in a hurry to get home—"

"That's 'cause he was trying to sneak in before I saw him, weren't you, boy?" Jacob accused his son angrily. "Think I don't know that you've been out drinking again? You're just rotting your liver a piece at a time, you know that, don't you?"

Trying to ignore his father's accusation, Bob looked at the sheriff. "Can I get back to work now?" he asked. "Billy and me still have to brand two more of the calves."

"Sure. Go back to work," Rick said. "And thanks for your help."

Rae didn't say anything until she, Sully and the sheriff got back into the sheriff's truck, although she could barely contain herself.

The second they were in the truck, it all came pouring out. "Rawlings said he never saw Warren come back from Murphy's that night. But Bob McGee said he saw someone in the bunkhouse when he dropped Wynters off there."

"Which means that one of them is lying," Sully said with finality.

"Unless there was someone else at the bunkhouse that night waiting for Wynters when he got back," Rick pointed out.

"That's a possibility," Rae allowed, then qualified, "except for one thing."

Both men looked at her.

"What?" Sully asked.

"Rawlings said he never left the bunkhouse all day, claiming that he really enjoyed the solitude," she reminded the two men.

The sheriff played devil's advocate. "He could have been lying."

"There was no reason to lie," Rae pointed out. "He probably assumed that Wynters drove himself back. He didn't know that someone else drove Wynters back to the bunkhouse and that the driver caught a glimpse of him when he dropped Wynters off."

"I'll bring him in for questioning," Rick told the other two occupants in the truck.

"No," Sully told him.

"No?" Rae questioned, confused. "Why not? Right now, everything points to Rawlings being the one who killed Wynters for the money. Or don't you think so?"

Sully nodded. "From where I'm standing, that sounds like a pretty safe bet," he said, wanting to make his thinking clear.

"Well, if you think that, why don't you want to bring him in?" Rae asked.

"Give him a few days," Sully advised. "We'll have people watching him. If he did it for the money, it's probably hidden somewhere. If we grab him up now, we might not be able to get him to admit to anything. But if we watch him, odds are that sooner or later, Rawlings is either going to want to check on the money just to reassure himself that it's still there—

or he might decide to get out of town quick, in which case he's going to pack up the money.

"Either way, he'll lead us to the money. But only," Sully emphasized, "if he doesn't think that we're onto him."

"What if he doesn't lead us back to the money?" Rae asked. "What if he decided to wait indefinitely? Just how long are you willing to play the waiting game?"

Sully laughed softly. "Look at Rawlings," he told her. "Does he strike you as someone who's willing to wait six months to a year—or longer—before he takes the money and runs?"

"He does have a point," Rick agreed.

Rae frowned. This whole case had her feeling itchy. Not to mention that she didn't really want to have to work alongside Rawlings, thinking that he was responsible for killing someone.

Even an embezzler deserved better than that, she thought.

"So you're saying we wait," she concluded, looking at Sully.

Instead of answering her, Sully looked at the sheriff. "What do you say, Sheriff?"

Rick had already made up his mind after hearing Sully out. "I think you're right," he told Sully. "I say we wait."

Rae sighed. "Then I guess we wait," she echoed, resigned to the fact.

But she wasn't happy about it.

Chapter 20

"Boy, I gotta say that I'm glad things are finally going to get back to the way they were," Rawlings said to Rae the following morning.

After some last-minute exchange of information and preparation was made, Roy Washburn left with the ranch hand he'd brought with him, heading back to the family ranch.

Watching them leave, Rawlings was positively beaming. Rae couldn't recall ever seeing the wrangler looking this happy since Miss Joan had sent him to the ranch over four months ago.

"I guess I never really appreciated how you ran the J-H until Washburn was here, barking out orders like some damn dictator," Rawlings confessed.

"Is that so?" Rae asked as she served breakfast

to Rawlings and Sully. She set down the last serving for herself.

"Yeah, you bet," Rawlings said with what amounted to enthusiasm, not bothering to swallow before he continued talking. "Washburn couldn't stop ordering me and the other guy around. But no matter what he did, the guy just couldn't hold a candle to you."

As he talked, the man made short work of the scrambled eggs and ham on his plate.

Rae wasn't fooled by the wrangler for a minute. Rawlings was laying it on really thick, being far more flattering than he ever had in all the time that he'd spent working on the J-H Ranch.

The man was up to something, most likely trying to get her off her guard.

She supposed that there was a slim chance that it could all be on the level, that Rawlings had realized how tough a foreman could be and appreciated the laid-back way that she usually ran the ranch.

It could be...

But, thinking about it for a moment, Rae really doubted it. Something in her gut just wouldn't allow her to give the other man a pass, especially in light of the way the ranch hand had behaved previously.

Maybe she wasn't being fair, but she couldn't help feeling that this was all an act, a cover, and that Rawlings was just biding his time until it was safe for him to grab the money—wherever he might have hidden it—and run.

Looking at Sully sitting across from her at the

table, she could see that the detective felt the same way she did.

They just had to wait until Rawlings made his move.

But waiting was going to be hell.

Things settled back to a routine, the same routine that had been followed when there had only been three of them on the ranch, Rae and the two ranch hands who had worked for her before Sully had joined their ranks. Now it was Sully working with them instead of Warren/Wynters.

Work seemed to be getting done faster. Oddly enough, Rawlings was now working harder, more diligently now that Warren/Wynters was gone—he was no longer trying to cut corners or finding excuses not to do something.

Even though Rawlings appeared to have undergone a transformation, Rae couldn't shake the feeling that she was sitting on a powder keg, waiting for it to suddenly blow up.

Hopefully not right under her.

By the time the fourth day under these conditions had come and gone, Rae could feel herself growing progressively more antsy. What she was afraid of was that this could turn into an endless waiting game.

"Maybe I was wrong," Rae told Sully, keeping her voice low as she brought in a bag of fresh feed for the horses.

"About Rawlings being responsible?" Sully asked, taking the bag from her.

Personally, Sully was suffering no such bouts of indecision. He was certain that the man they were watching was the guilty party, even though the partial fingerprints he'd managed to secure and send off to Valri hadn't yielded a criminal record or an alias.

"No, about his being able to stretch this game of his out until he feels secure enough to take off with the money. Apparently, he's more patient than I thought." She looked at Sully. "If you were him, where would you hide the money?"

"A lot of places come to mind," he answered. Opening the bag, he began distributing the feed in the different stalls. "We could easily spend the next six months tossing every square inch of this ranch without finding it."

She made sure that none of the stalls had been overlooked. She glanced toward Sully. "I thought you were an optimist."

"No, I'm a realist. Don't worry, Rachel," he assured her, his voice softening, "Rawlings is going to slip up. The sheriff's got his deputies taking turns watching the bunkhouse at night in case Rawlings decides to sneak off with the money then. And I'm keeping an eye on him during the day."

Rae sighed. "Yeah, me, too." But that didn't alleviate her restless feeling.

All in all, Rae had to admit to herself that she had mixed feelings about all this. On the one hand, she had a real desire to prove that Rawlings had been the one who'd killed Wynters. The first step was to

catch the ranch hand making off with the money that
Wynters had stolen from his employer.

But on the other hand, she knew that once that
happened, once they had their proof and caught
Rawlings red-handed, then this would all be over.
Sully would go back to his home and to his life in
California. There'd be no more need for him to re-
main here.

The quiet, withdrawn man he'd been when he first
arrived was gone now. He'd disappeared completely
the second he had stumbled across Wynters's buried
body. It was obvious that Sully Cavanaugh *thrived*
on being a detective, on solving crimes and putting
perpetrators away. As a rule, that kind of a thing
didn't happen here. It was waiting for him back in
California.

Thinking about that caused a huge knot to form
and grow right in the pit of her stomach no matter
how much she struggled to ignore it.

"Maybe I should move into the bunkhouse," Sully
said a few days later. He'd been thinking out loud
while he and Rae were attempting to saddle break
one of the yearlings.

The comment had come out of the blue and caught
her totally off guard. She forgot about the yearling
for a moment.

"Why?" she asked.

"Well, that way I could keep a closer eye on Rawlings. With me there, there's no doubt that he'll feel
hemmed in. Maybe he'll take off sooner, leaving

when he thinks I'm asleep. It could be just the thing to get this to move forward."

Here she was, feeling torn again. Sully had a point, but did she really want this to move any faster than it was?

"Rick's deputies are taking turns watching the bunkhouse," she reminded him.

"Having an extra set of eyes on Rawlings close up wouldn't hurt," Sully told her.

Rae knew she should just agree and go along with it. Anyone remotely interested in bringing this matter to a close would have approved of Sully's idea.

"I don't want you to move into the bunkhouse," she told him.

Sully had only half heard her, and what he heard didn't make sense. He blinked, replaying her words in his head. They still didn't make any sense.

"What?"

"I don't want you to move into the bunkhouse," she repeated more firmly. "I want you to stay where you are," she told him, her eyes meeting his. "With me," she added, her voice lowering.

He looked at her for a long moment, and for the life of her, Rae couldn't begin to guess what Sully was thinking.

And then his mouth curved slightly. "I guess I'm not in a position to disregard the foreman."

Rae knew she was interfering with the case. Knew, too, that she had no right to do that, but she didn't care. She wanted to hang on to the little bit of sunshine she'd found in her life for as long as she could. It would be gone all too soon, and they both knew it.

"Damn straight you're not," she whispered to him. Glancing around to see if anyone was watching them—she included the deputy as well as Rawlings, and neither one seemed to be—she allowed herself one tiny moment of freedom and kissed Sully.

Rae pulled back before Sully could deepen the kiss because she knew if he did, she would wind up making love with him right here and now in one of the horse stalls. She was not about to jeopardize everything Sully was striving to do just for the fleeing satisfaction of being with him one more time, at least not unless it was behind closed doors.

That night, it was.

Sully lay beside her in her room when their lovemaking was over. Each time they did it, it seemed to get more aggressive than the last time. He found that catching his breath was proving to be a little more challenging each time they made love.

Turning his face toward Rae, he said, "You really wear me out, Mulcahy. I'm not sure I can keep up with you after putting in a full day's work." Reluctantly, he rose and pulled on his jeans. He wanted to be prepared just in case he had to move fast.

But all he really wanted to do was stay in bed with her.

Ever leery of having all this end at a moment's notice, fear spread an icy blanket over her.

"Is that your way of saying you don't want to do this anymore?" she asked him.

Her question surprised him. "No," he told her, crossing over to where he had tossed off his boots, "that's my way of saying that that I'm going to need to look into buying some vitamins," he said with a disparaging laugh.

And then, glancing out the window and catching a movement out of the corner of his eye, he froze.

Rae had just thrown on the oversize shirt she slept in. Seeing the look on Sully's face, she instantly asked, "What's wrong?"

"Gabe's on the ground. Rawlings just knocked him out." Sully tossed the words over his shoulder as he ran from the room and down the stairs.

After grabbing her jeans, she pulled them on while following right behind Sully. She was running before his words had even sunk in.

On the first floor, she paused only long enough to grab something from the side table before flying out the door in Sully's wake.

Sully ran to the bunkhouse. Rawlings was gone. Gabe was lying unconscious, facedown on the ground. Sully saw that there was a gash on the back of the man's head.

Just like there'd been with Wynters.

Blood was pouring out of the deputy's wound.

Sully felt for a pulse. He breathed a sigh of relief when he found one. It wasn't strong, but it was definitely there.

Reaching into his pocket for his cell phone, he quickly called the sheriff.

"Santiago."

"We were right. Rawlings made his move. He knocked Gabe out. Gabe needs medical attention."

"Where are you?" Rick demanded. From the sound of his voice, Sully guessed that the man was hurrying to his vehicle.

"In front of the bunkhouse. I saw Rawlings taking off after hitting Gabe's head with something heavy." He looked down at the deputy. "Probably with the same thing he used on Wynters."

"I'm on my way," Rick told him, adding, "I'll grab the doc."

The call terminated.

Only when Sully turned to tuck his phone back into his pocket did he realize Rae was gone.

"Damn it, woman," Sully cursed, frustrated.

He couldn't just leave the unconscious deputy out here bleeding, but he didn't have a good feeling about this.

Rae had gone to bring Rawlings in.

She was playing a hunch. Rawlings had shown time and again that he wasn't much of a woodsman. It had rained yesterday, not hard, but enough. A lot of the roads were still muddy, which meant that the fleeing murderer would leave a trail that even a myopic five-year-old could follow.

Rawlings had already killed one man, and for all she knew, he could have just killed another. She was not about to let him get away with it if she could help it.

He had to be stopped.

The money didn't matter to her. It wasn't about the money, although she didn't approve of stealing. However, wantonly killing another human being mattered a great deal to her. She couldn't just let him get away. Rawlings worked on the ranch she oversaw, which to her meant that she was responsible for him and for everything he did while he worked for her.

She needed to catch him before someone else inadvertently cornered him and Rawlings wound up killing someone else—maybe even Sully—in order to get away.

She forced herself to block out everything except focusing on catching Rawlings.

Desperate to get away, Rawlings was fleeing in his truck. But the terrain was uneven and hilly, made that much harder to traverse because of the mud. And it was raining again.

She guessed at his escape route, following the newly made tracks. Because the road was so hard to navigate, Rae pursued the inept ranch hand on horseback.

She made better time than he did.

It didn't take her long to catch up to him. She saw him up ahead. His truck had gotten stuck in the mud.

A whining noise grew louder, alerting her that the vehicle wasn't going anywhere. Its front wheels were only managing to get deeper and deeper embedded in the mud.

Rae dismounted, leaving her horse as she drew closer to Rawlings. Fixated on the truck's dilemma, he was oblivious to her presence.

"Going somewhere?" Rae asked, raising her voice above the sound of the engine.

Startled, Rawlings glared at her, cursing and telling her what she could do with her question.

The sound of a handgun being cocked registered above the truck's noise. It stopped him mid-curse.

The weapon was the one thing she had thought to grab before she flew after Sully when he left the house.

She had it trained now on Rawlings. "Get out of the car," she ordered.

"You're not going to shoot me," Rawlings taunted haughtily.

The next second, he let loose a guttural shriek that telegraphed his fear, and he winced as he automatically ducked. Rae had sent a bullet whizzing by exceedingly close to his right ear.

"I wouldn't bet on it if I were you," Rae calmly told the ranch hand. "The one thing Miss Joan did before putting me in charge of this ranch was make sure I learned how to shoot anything with a trigger and how to get whatever I aimed for. In this case, I was aiming just to the right of your ear. But I can aim closer if you'd like that instead."

Rawlings was visibly shaking now. "I'll give you half," he told her, never taking his eyes off the gun in her hand. "There's a lot of money in these bags of his, and I'll give you half of everything if you just let me drive out of here."

She couldn't believe that he had actually said that. How depraved did he think she was?

"Sorry, no deal," she told him.

"Okay," he cried breathlessly, his eyes wild as he tried to think. "I'll give you all of it. *All of it*," he stressed. "If you just let me go. Think about it. All that money. Think what you could do with it. You could live like a queen."

"I never wanted to be a queen," she told him in a flat, uninterested voice. The rain was making the nightshirt she'd thrown on stick to her body. She didn't make for a frightening figure. "I'm taking you in for Jefferson Wynters's murder."

He looked totally confused. "Who the hell is that?" Rawlings asked.

"That's the man you knew as John Warren," she told him. "The man you killed so you could steal the money that *he* stole."

He was beginning to resemble a caged animal looking for a way out. "I didn't kill him," Rawlings protested.

She wasn't about to get into this with him. "He looked pretty dead to me."

Rawlings was breathing harder now. As he spoke, he tried to move closer to her. "That was an accident. He tripped, fell backward and hit his head on a rock."

"And the stab wounds?" Rae asked. "Were they an accident, too?"

Rawlings had the look of a man who knew he was

cornered. Who knew that he had absolutely nothing to lose. With another gut-wrenching cry that sounded more animal-like than human, Rawlings ducked his head down and lunged for Rae like a football player executing a desperate tackle to block what looked like the winning play.

He caught Rae off guard, knocking the gun out of her hand. It went flying at the same time that he had knocked the air right out of her lungs.

"You stupid bitch! You just couldn't leave it alone, could you?" he cried.

He whirled around to grab the gun from the ground.

Chapter 21

Rawlings scrambled up, the gun clutched in his hand. Adrenaline shot through him as he took a step a couple of steps back and aimed the gun at Rae, dead center.

His eyes seemed to glow as he announced, "Guess it's time for you to say goodbye, you no-good—"

Rawlings didn't get to finish his sentence. Instead, a round of curses emerged. They mingled with the sound of gunfire and some indistinguishable shriek of pain as a bullet pierced Rawlings's shoulder. Falling to his knees, the ranch hand dropped the handgun.

The man's head spun around like a top as he tried to figure out what had just happened and who had fired at him.

The next second, Rawlings didn't have to wonder. He had his answer.

Keeping his weapon trained on Rawlings, Sully quickly made his way over to Rae.

Rae struggled to get back to her feet. "I don't think I've ever been so glad to see you," she cried.

"What the hell were you thinking, taking off like that?" Sully demanded, his eyes still on Rawlings, but he allowed himself a second to quickly look over Rae to check her for any wounds.

Rae pretended to frown. "Maybe I should rethink what I just said," she amended.

But he wasn't about to engage in any banter. He was furious—and Rae had scared him to death with her disappearing act.

"He almost killed you!" Sully snapped, the vivid scenario of what *could* have happened playing itself over and over in his head.

"I was trying to keep him from killing anyone else," she retorted, speaking up in her own defense.

"But you were supposed to wait for backup," he informed her angrily. "You know that."

A fake smile curved her mouth. "Where's your backup?" she asked.

About to retort an answer, Sully suddenly cocked his weapon, bringing everyone's attention back to the immediate scenario. The ranch hand had started to inch away, apparently hoping that Rae would distract the other man long enough for him to get away.

Sully's eyebrows narrowed. "You take one more step and you'll have to learn how to walk without legs because I'll break them—and then I'll show you what happens when I *really* get angry," he threatened evenly.

"All right, all right," Rawlings cried, raising his hands up over his head.

Rae released a shaky breath, willing herself to relax. It had been touch and go for a few moments there. "How did you find me?" she asked Sully.

He spared her a look. He wanted to hug her to him, but that would have to wait until he'd taken care of Rawlings.

"I followed his car tracks, same as you. You're not the only one who knows how to track, you know," Sully informed her.

He turned his attention exclusively to Rawlings. Taking out a pair of handcuffs, he told the wrangler, "Put your hands behind your back." When Rawlings refused, Sully pulled his hands back for him. Snapping the cuffs on the man, Sully said, "Jack Rawlings, you're under arrest for the murder of Jefferson Wynters and the attempted murders of Deputy Gabriel Rodriguez and Rachel Mulcahy."

"I didn't kill anyone!" Rawlings shouted, trying to yank his hands away.

But the effort was fruitless.

"I'm not arguing with you. Get in the car—the back seat of the car," Sully emphasized when it looked as if Rawlings was going to get in on the passenger side in the front of the vehicle. Moving quickly, Sully secured the man in his seat.

"And you get in the front," he proceeded to tell Rae.

She glanced over to where the horse she'd ridden was standing. "I'll ride Starlight back," she began to tell Sully.

He cut her off. "The hell you will. I'm not taking a chance on you suddenly getting dizzy and falling off the horse because this lowlife hit your head."

"I can't just leave Starlight here," she protested.

He knew there was no arguing her out of this. "We'll tie the horse's reins onto the rear of the truck—don't worry, I'll drive slow," he said, anticipating her next protest. "Although," he amended, wrinkling his nose in disgust as he hauled out the bags of money that Rawlings had stashed in his truck, "this smell is enough to make me go as fast as possible."

Suddenly getting a pungent whiff, Rae nearly gagged.

"What *is* that smell?" she cried, startled. And even as she asked, it came to her.

Sully had already figured it out, as well as where Wynters had hidden the bags of money and why no one had found them. The smell was very distinct.

"*That's* why no one found where Wynters hid the money." He looked at his prisoner in the back seat. "You saw him digging up the money the night of the party, didn't you?" It wasn't a question. The smell on the bags was strong enough to erase all doubt. Sully glanced toward Rae. "The money was hidden in the bins of fertilizer. No one wants to sink their hands in manure unless they absolutely have to," he told her. He had to give Wynters his due as far as resourcefulness went. "Actually, that was pretty clever," Sully conceded.

Rae was doing her best to only take shallow breaths. "Also disgusting," she added.

"Yeah, that, too," Sully agreed with a laugh.

Securing Starlight's reins to the rear of his truck, Sully got in behind the wheel. All four of the windows were down.

This was going to be a long trip, he thought.

"Sure took you guys long enough to get here," the sheriff declared. The sound of the approaching truck had alerted him, and he'd left his office to meet Sully and Rae *and* their prisoner. "I was just about to go looking out for you. I figured something must have happened."

"Mulcahy here cornered Rawlings on horseback," Sully explained, getting out of the truck. On the other side, Rae had done the same. "I tied the horse's reins to the back end of the truck and didn't want to take a chance on having him collapse trying to keep up," he explained.

"Hey, you don't owe me any explanations after catching Wynters's killer," Rick told him.

"Hey, what about me?" Rawlings cried. "This smell is sickening!"

Moving to the rear of the truck, Sully yanked the prisoner out. "Actually, it was a joint effort," he told the sheriff, deliberately ignoring Rawlings complaints. "Mulcahy here got the drop on him. I just provided backup."

Sully's narrative surprised her. But she never took credit for things she felt she wasn't due. "Sully provided more than just backup, Sheriff."

But Rick stopped her right there. "It's late, you two. I'm not in the mood to try to play Solomon here. We'll sort it all out in the morning. I just want this lowlife behind bars," he informed them.

Taking hold of the protesting Rawlings, he marched him into his office. Heading to the rear of the station, he brought him to the jail cell, which rarely saw any traffic. When it did, it was usually one of the two town drunks, there to sleep it off before going home.

Rawlings was the first killer to be housed within the cell.

The door was locked despite Rawlings's vehement protest.

"How's Gabe?" Rae asked once Rawlings was secured and the money locked up in the sheriff's rarely used safe.

The sheriff laughed. "Madder than a wet hen just about now," he told them. "The doc patched him up. I figure a couple of days' bed rest, he'll be better than new. Gabe's got a hard head. It takes more than having a rock thrown at it to cause any damage. Speaking of which," Rick said, taking a closer look at Rae. "You look like you didn't fare all that well in the confrontation you had. Rawlings?"

Rae waved her hand at his question. "I'm okay," she said dismissively.

Sully acted as if she hadn't said anything. "I'll bring her over to the doc," he told the sheriff.

Rick nodded. "I was just about to suggest that," he said. "Davenport's waiting for you at the clinic. He kept the doors open."

Taking her hand firmly in his, Sully escorted her out of the sheriff's office. "I'll see you in the morning," Sully promised the sheriff.

Having whisked Rae into his truck, he drove her over to the medical clinic.

Arriving there, he got out quickly and rounded the front of the truck. He opened the door on the passenger side, but before Rae could step out, he picked her up in his arms. Holding her, Sully closed the door using his back.

"What are you doing?" she demanded.

She made one attempt to get Sully to put her down, but when that effort failed, she realized that she felt a little too weak to attempt walking into the clinic on her own.

"Practicing," he said, answering her question.

"Practicing?" she repeated, confused. "Practicing for what?"

His grin looked lopsided. "You ask too many questions," he told her.

Going up the steps to the clinic, he didn't have to knock. Dan was waiting for them.

"Last exam room," he told the duo.

Rae picked up her conversation as if there'd been no pause.

"That's because you never answer anything," she

insisted. "Like with Rawlings. You never explained how you managed to track him down. You're from the big city," she pointed out, not buying his tracking explanation.

"Yeah, and I spent every summer hunting with my grandfather," he told her.

She shook her head. "I'm having trouble visualizing you shooting animals."

"That's because we didn't," he told her. "We just hunted them. Once we tracked the animal down, we went on to another challenge. It was tracking the game that was exhilarating. Tracking sharpened a lot of skills."

"Well, I for one am glad you sharpened them. Otherwise, Doc here would be in his bed right about now, getting some much-deserved sleep," she said, looking around Sully's arm at the doctor.

Dan looked at Sully. "Was that a veiled expression of gratitude or a put-down?" he asked, amused.

"I honestly couldn't tell you," Sully said as he walked down the corridor. "She takes a lot of figuring out."

"Good luck with that," the doctor told him with a laugh. "I'm still trying to figure out mine."

"Hey, you two, I was banged up," Rae protested, speaking up. "I didn't lose my hearing."

"We'll be sure to keep that in mind," Dan told her. "Last room, Sully," he repeated.

"On our way," Sully responded.

"I can walk," Rae protested.

"I know, but humor me," Sully said, smiling at her. "There's less resistance this way."

Reaching the room, he went inside and deposited her on the exam table. She expected him to step back, but he remained right beside her. Did he expect her to make a break for it? she wondered.

"Are you up on your tetanus injections?" Dan asked.

She paused, trying to remember the last time she'd received one.

Dan nodded, as if conducting his own internal conversation. He had his answer.

"If you have to think that long, then it's been *too* long. I'll give you a booster. I have to get the serum from the front room," he told them. "Stay right here. I'll be right back." In the doorway, Dan gave her a pseudo-warning look. "Stay put, all right?"

Restless, edgy, Rae shifted a little on the exam table. Sully moved closer to her. "You heard what the doc said."

"I'm staying put," Rae protested. Saying the words reminded her that he'd be doing just the opposite now that he'd caught Wynters's killer. She felt a sadness spreading out within her. "But you're not."

His brow furrowed as if he didn't know what she was talking about. "I'm right here," he pointed out.

"No, I mean in Forever," she told him. "Now that you found the killer and the money, the case is solved. There's no reason for you to stay here any longer."

She'd seen the look on his face. He thrived on this

kind of challenge. And Forever averaged a case of this magnitude once in a lifetime. Sully would be bored out of his mind inside a week.

"Are you kicking me out, Mulcahy?" Sully asked her innocently.

"No, of course not." But she couldn't very well tie him up, either, Rae thought. "I just know when something's over."

"Well, my dad always told us that when one door closes, another one opens." She continued looking at him, waiting for him to make his point. "I'm not exactly a math wizard, but I'd say that you're two ranch hands short right now."

She still didn't understand what he was saying— and she was afraid to jump to any conclusions because the disappointment would be too great.

"Wynters is dead and Rawlings is going away for his murder, so I'd say your math was pretty good," she told him, "but—"

Patiently, Sully tried again. "Didn't you mention that this was your busy season? Something about those yearlings needing to be saddle broke and trained?" he asked.

Her eyes never left his as a kernel of hope popped somewhere within her.

"I said that, but…"

Sully pretended to pick up on the word *but*.

"Then you *don't* need help?"

"Of course I need help," she cried, "but…"

He didn't let her get any further. The woman definitely talked too much.

"Then I'll stay and help," Sully said. "Unless you don't want me to."

"It's not a matter of my not wanting you to do something," she protested. He had a career and a family waiting for him. "It's—"

Sully cut her short. "Fine, then it's settled." Moving a wayward strand of her hair from her face, he grinned. "I'll stay."

She blew out a frustrated breath. "Are you *ever* going to allow me to finish a sentence?" she asked.

There was an amused, teasing look in his eyes. "That all depends."

"On what?" she asked. The man was making her crazy, she thought.

As he stood there, looking at her, his eyes were all but making love to her.

"On whether or not it's going to be something I want to hear," he answered.

She could feel laughter bubbling up inside her. But she tried not to let it surface just yet. Not until they were really alone together. "You certainly do have a lot of conditions."

Sully laughed, amused. "I'm a Cavanaugh. It comes with the territory. Now stop trying to change the topic. Do you want me to stay and help out until after you finish up with those yearlings?"

"Of course I want you to stay." *To work with all my yearlings from this day on.* "But your family probably needs you back."

"My family's flexible," he assured her, taking her

hand in his. "I'll stay to help out, and once that's done…we'll see," he told her.

"Okay if I come back in now?" Dan asked, looking from one to the other. "Is the debate about whether he stays or goes over?" the doctor asked as he came into the room a little farther.

"Of course you can come in. Sorry, didn't want to make you think you needed to wait to get in one of your own exam rooms," Sully apologized.

"Sounded like pretty much of a life-or-death conversation to me," Dan said, washing his hands again and putting on a fresh pair of light blue gloves. "All right," he said, turning around to face Rae. The doctor picked up the syringe. "Are you ready for this?"

She slanted a look toward Sully and for once didn't suppress the smile that rose to her lips. "I'm ready for anything," she told him.

Sully did his best to suppress the laughter he felt building within him—until they were alone together.

"You heard the lady, Doc," he said, his eyes on Rae's.

"Then let's get started," Dan urged his patient.

She looked at Sully, and for a second, their eyes met and held.

"I think that maybe I already have," she said in a voice that was only loud enough for Sully to hear.

Epilogue

It seemed to her like there were Cavanaughs, either by birth or by marriage, in every single nook and cranny within the spacious two-story house and its extensive backyard. They'd all turned out to welcome Sully back. His uncle Andrew was throwing the party for him, Sully told her as if it was no big deal.

And to him, it wasn't. He took things like this for granted, she thought. She'd never had the opportunity to take anything like this for granted, because for her there had been no parties.

She'd been apprehensive about meeting these people when he told her about the party, but within the first few minutes at his uncle's house, they had somehow managed to put her at ease.

All of them.

To a person.

Her apprehension melted away as if it had never even existed. She started to enjoy herself after that.

In truth, time seemed to just fly by even as she savored every moment.

"Well, what do you think?" Sully asked Rae when he could finally pull her aside some five hours into the party.

"I think you have more family than any ten people I know," she said wistfully.

Sully laughed. "You're probably right. At the time, it felt really good to get away. I needed to," he confided. "But it feels even better now to get back here."

There was something to make her smile everywhere she looked. Smile and at the same time feel envious of the man beside her.

"If I were you," she told him, "I would have never left."

"It wasn't my family that was the problem," Sully reminded her. "It was the work."

"The case you were working," Rae corrected. "But all that's behind you. And watching you back in Forever, hunting for Wynters and then his killer, just shows me that no matter what you say, police work is in your blood. Just like the Cavanaughs are," she added with a smile, glancing around the immediate area. There were so many different faces, she felt overwhelmed. "How do you remember all their names?" she marveled, trying to recall the names of the couple in the corner and drawing a blank.

"Gradually. It's work," he admitted. "But it's a labor of love."

She smiled, watching as Andrew paused to brush a kiss on his wife, Rose's, cheek in passing. "You don't know how lucky you are," Rae told him softly, still scanning the crowd.

"Oh, I think I know," Sully said, looking at her.

"I'm really going to miss this when I go back," she said honestly.

"Then why don't you stay a little longer?" Sully asked. He looked at her hopefully.

She really wanted to, but she felt she couldn't. Miss Joan was counting on her. "I asked Miss Joan for a week off, and it's been a week. I can't just leave her high and dry like that."

"Well, maybe not so high or dry," Sully speculated.

She looked at him, puzzled. "What are you talking about?"

"Well, I talked to Miss Joan, too," he told her, slowly feeling his way around the subject he was about to broach. "I asked her if she had any contingency plans."

"Contingency plans?" Rae repeated. It made no more sense to her the second time than the first. "What kind of a contingency are you talking about?"

He threaded his fingers through hers. "Like if you took longer getting back than you initially thought— and she said yes, by the way."

"She said yes," Rae echoed, still somewhat mystified.

"That she had a contingency plan," he prompted.

"And exactly what do those plans involve?" Rae asked.

"She'd get Roy Washburn back to run the ranch. He did really well while we were otherwise engaged," he reminded her, "and Miss Joan thinks he's itching to run a place on his own, without his brother looking over his shoulder all the time."

"So if I stayed an extra week, everyone would be okay with that?" Rae asked uncertainly.

Sully grinned at her. "Absolutely."

She played it out a little further. "How about if I decided to stay a month?"

"That, too," Sully told her with slightly more enthusiasm.

Rae rolled it over in her mind. "Well, it wouldn't be for a month," she decided, half talking to herself.

Sully looked at her, alert. "Why not?" he asked.

She thought the answer to that was self-evident. "I wouldn't want to wear out my welcome," she told Sully.

Right before her eyes, Sully's smile turned downright sexy.

"Oh, you wouldn't wear out your welcome in a month," he assured her. "Maybe in fifty years, but not anything less than that."

Rae laughed, thinking he was making a joke. "Now you're just teasing me."

"No," Sully answered quietly, his eyes meeting hers. "I'm not."

"What are you saying?" Rae asked, afraid to allow her imagination to run away with her.

He looked at her for a long moment. And then he could have sworn that he heard Miss Joan's voice in his head, telling him to *Man up, boy, and speak your piece. Tell her what's in your heart. You owe that to her. She's not a mind reader, you know.*

Right as always, Miss Joan, he thought.

Taking her hand, he drew Rae over to the only area that for the moment was not overflowing with members of his family.

"What I'm saying is that I don't want you to go," he told her. "I asked you to come out here with me for an ulterior motive," he admitted.

"What motive?" she asked, confused.

"To see how you'd react to my family. To see if you like them," he said honestly.

"You thought I wouldn't like them?" she asked incredulously. "*These* people? When I was a little girl, it was just my dad and me. I used to pray all the time that one day a family would just somehow magically appear. A family that my dad had just forgotten he had. But he hadn't and it didn't—and then I lost him, too, and wound up alone.

"Meeting your family and pretending, just for a moment, that they were my family, is like hitting some sort of an impossible jackpot," she told him. And then, replaying her words in her head, she waved them away. "You probably think I'm crazy."

"No, I don't," Sully told her. "And you don't have to pretend that they're your family—"

She felt her color rising to her cheeks. "I know, I'm sorry. I shouldn't—"

She tried to turn away, but he caught both of her hands in his, drawing her around. "Because they can be your family—if you're willing to put up with me."

She heard the words, but they weren't registering. It was too good to be true—she had to have missed something. "What are you saying?" she asked in disbelief.

"I'm stumbling through a proposal. *Stumbling* being the operative word here," he told her. He took a breath and plunged in. "I'm not any good at this because I've never done this before. Maybe if I practice—"

Her eyes widened, and she cried, "Yes!"

He thought she was telling him to try again. "All right then, from the top—"

She shook her head. He didn't understand. "No!"

Now he was completely confused. "Then you *don't* want me to propose?"

"No." She pressed her hand against her chest as if that would somehow still her hammering heart. "You don't have to propose again," she told him. "Because I'll marry you."

"Because I have family to spare?" he asked with a grin.

"Because every time you kiss me, you make the world fade away. Because you make me feel loved and safe. And because you make me want to make you feel the same way."

"You already do," he told her, taking her into his arms.

She'd never felt so happy in her whole life. Every inch of her felt as if it was smiling. "I guess all that's left to do is for me to call Miss Joan and tell her that I've decided to stay here."

Holding her to him, Sully looked down into her face. "Between you and me, I think she already figured that part out."

She knew he was right. Miss Joan always knew everything before it happened. "I wonder if she'd like to be my matron of honor."

"You know, I think she's counting on it," Sully told her.

He had an announcement to make, but first, just for a minute, he wanted to have Rae to himself.

And, lowering his mouth to hers, he did.

* * * * *

*Don't forget previous titles in the
Cavanaugh Justice series:*

Cavanaugh's Secret Delivery
Cavanaugh Vanguard
Cavanaugh Encounter
Cavanaugh on Call
Cavanaugh in the Rough

Available now from Harlequin Romantic Suspense!

Before she could decide, Spence wrapped his arm around her
shoulder, yanking her against his side.

"Mia yelped.

So much tension shot through his body that she could feel it
seeping into her own muscles.

"What're you doing?"

"Using you as camouflage," he said, looking away from his
prey just long enough to give her a smile.

"The guy ran from me once already. I don't want him getting
away again."

"Again? What do you mean, again?" He wasn't going to chase
the man through this building, was he?

"He crashed your party last week to confront Alcosta, and now
he's at the man's office. If the guy means trouble, what do you
think the chances are that he wouldn't show up again at one of your
Alcosta fund-raisers?"

Mia frowned.

Well, that burst her sexy little fantasy.

"Are you sure it's the same guy?"

Taking her cue from Spence, instead of twisting around to
check the other man out this time, Mia dropped her purse so that

when she bent down to pick it up, she could look over without being obvious.

It was the same man, all right.

And he wore the same dark scowl.

"He looks mean," she murmured.

The man was about her height, but almost as broad as Spence. Even in a pricey suit, his muscles rippled in a way that screamed brawler. Cell phone against his ear, he paced in front of the elevator, enough anger in his steps that she was surprised he didn't kick the metal doors to hurry it up.

"I'm going to follow him, see where he goes."

"No," Mia protested. "He could be dangerous."

"So can I."

Oh, God.

Why did that turn her on?

"Maybe you should call security instead of following him," she suggested. She knew the words were futile before they even left her lips, but she'd had to try.

"No point." He wrapped her fingers around her portfolio. "Wait for me in front of the building."

"Hold on." She made a grab for him, but his sport coat slipped through her fingers. "Spence, please."

That stopped him.

He stopped and gave her an impatient look.

"This is what I do." He headed for the elevator without a backward glance, leaving Mia standing there, with worry crawling up and down her spine as she watched him check the elevator the guy had taken before hurrying to the stairwell.

Oh, damn.

Don't miss
Navy SEAL Bodyguard *by Tawny Weber,*
available June 2019 wherever
Harlequin® Romantic Suspense books
and ebooks are sold.

www.Harlequin.com

Need an adrenaline rush from nail-biting tales
(and irresistible males)?

Check out **Harlequin Intrigue®**,
Harlequin® Romantic Suspense and
Love Inspired® Suspense books!

New books available every month!

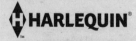

Love Harlequin romance?

DISCOVER.

Be the first to find out about promotions, news and exclusive content!

Facebook.com/HarlequinBooks

Twitter.com/HarlequinBooks

Instagram.com/HarlequinBooks

Pinterest.com/HarlequinBooks

ReaderService.com

EXPLORE.

Sign up for the Harlequin e-newsletter and download a free book from any series at **TryHarlequin.com.**

CONNECT.

Join our Harlequin community to share your thoughts and connect with other romance readers!
Facebook.com/groups/HarlequinConnection

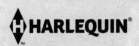

HARLEQUIN®

**ROMANCE WHEN
YOU NEED IT**

HSOCIAL2018

Reward the book lover in you!

Earn points on your purchase of new Harlequin books from participating retailers.

Turn your points into **FREE BOOKS** of your choice!

Join for FREE today at
www.HarlequinMyRewards.com.

Harlequin My Rewards is a free program (no fees) without any commitments or obligations.